# LOVE IS GRAND

Book 2 of the Grand Love Series

# LOVE IS GRAND

rachel
blaufeld

*Love Is Grand*
Copyright © 2022 Rachel Blaufeld
All rights reserved

Paperback ISBN-978-1-7340017-9-2

Edited by
Pam Berehulke

Proofread by
Virginia Tesi Carey

Cover design by
© Sarah Hansen, Okay Creations, LLC
www.okaycreations.com

Interior formatted by

emtippettsbookdesigns.com

This is a work of fiction. Names, characters, places, brands, media, and incidents are either the product of the author's imagination or are used fictitiously. The author acknowledges the trademarked status and trademark owners of various products referenced in this work of fiction, which have been used without permission. The publication/use of these trademarks is not authorized, associated with, or sponsored by the trademark owners.

**Warning:**

This book is intended for mature audiences.

*For my stepdad. We can all use a dream come true in our lives . . .*

# CHAPTER ONE

*Shell*

"You back there, Sam?"

When I heard the woman's voice coming from the front of Island Coffee, my dad's coffee shop, I wanted to hide in the back room forever. Taking my time to grab an extra milk, I was in no hurry to wait on the customer whose voice was all too familiar. The sound of it used to make me smile, but now, hearing it made me want to run away.

Keeping secrets would do that to you.

"Dad's not here," I called out, making my way up front to the counter.

"Oh, Shell, what's up? I haven't seen you in a while."

Rylan gave me a kind smile, but I didn't deserve her kindness.

My friend stood there, glistening from her run but looking as beautiful as ever. The thing was, it was hard to hate her because she didn't even know how gorgeous she was. Her smile was captivating when she chose to share it, and up until a couple of months ago, she'd been heartbroken. Now, her prince was back and living in the West Bay on the island.

Lucky girl . . . unlike me.

"You okay?" she asked, pulling me from my unhappy reverie.

"Yeah," I said. "Tired. Weezie is getting over a cold, and she's been coughing at night."

Knowing Rylan's usual order, I poured a large coffee and added milk.

"This is the Caribbean," she said. "We're not supposed to get colds."

I knew Rylan was kidding. Damn vacationers brought all kinds of viruses to the island.

"Exactly," I said, teasing back, hoping she'd get leave quickly.

Another thing about Rylan was she pretended to not get involved in people's lives, but she did. Especially mine. All. The. Time.

"Where's your dad?" she asked.

"Took my mom to the eye doctor. No biggie. She just can't drive after they dilate her eyes. Weezie went with them and is waiting in the car with my dad."

"No school?"

*Cripes*, Rylan was a nosy one.

"Parent/teacher conference day. So, nope."

She nodded. "These kids have it made. She's in what, kindergarten now?"

I nodded.

Leaning on the counter with her coffee next to her, Rylan gave me an odd look. "So, how are you, Shell? I mean, really?"

Wiping my hands on my apron, I averted my gaze.

"Shell?"

"It's been tough," I said, keeping busy so I didn't have to look my friend in the eye. "Weez misses her dad. As for me, I just wish he'd burn in hell for leaving us like he did. Sorry to say."

"Of course you do. Ricky is slime, but you're a better woman and the best mom."

I shook my head. "I'm messing it all up."

"Nah," Rylan said, waving off my concerns. "No way. Plus, Tony is crazy for you."

"We're just friends," I said a little too defensively.

I was my own worst enemy. Here I was wanting Rylan to ask less, and yet I was leaving little bread crumbs for her to follow a path straight to the truth.

Rylan tilted her head, studying me. "Tony would be good to you. He's a nice guy."

"Look, he's great, and I know you two are best friends, but now isn't a good time for me to get involved like that."

Except, I was involved, but with someone else. Someone more complicated, and much worse for me than Tony.

"I hear you," Rylan said softly. "But you're not alone, Shell. I'm here. Teddi loves you. Reach out."

"By the way, you didn't run here from the new house, did you?"

Everyone knew Rylan's guy, Adam, had bought a huge house in the West Bay. He'd decided to live here for most of the year, traveling back and forth to the States, wooing her along the way. Of course, she'd moved in with him.

"No, I came in early to work to check on a delivery, took a run, and now I'm going back to work."

"You're still bartending?"

"Yep, but I start my new gig in a few weeks. I'm nervous I won't like it, but this will let me travel back to the US with Adam. He only has a three-month visitor's visa now."

I knew what Adam wanted because he'd told Dad, but I was pretty sure Rylan was in denial.

"Do I hear wedding bells?" I asked, pleased to see Rylan looking uncomfortable instead of me.

"Uh, no."

"We'll see."

With that, Rylan stood tall and finished her coffee. "I gotta jog back and get a shower. Are you free this Friday, or do you work?"

Actually, I had the night off at the restaurant, and my parents were taking Weezie, so I was totally free. I'd planned to take a bath and read a book, but I wasn't about to tell Rylan that yet.

"Why?" I asked warily.

Rylan smiled. "We're going to have some cocktails and apps. Can you escape and come?"

"Oh, that sounds so nice," I said, unable to control my desire to have some adult time.

Then Rylan dropped the bomb.

"Cal's flying in. Adam wants him to have a good time since he's shouldering a lot of the workload. Which I know is BS, but you know Adam. He's always indebted to his family."

Sadly, after she said Cal's name, everything else sounded like gibberish as my brain fought to find an excuse for begging off on Friday.

Rylan must not have noticed because she said, "See you around seven," flicking her ponytail and then hurrying out the door.

The chimes tingling above the door after she left didn't even bring me out of my haze.

*Cripes.* Cal was coming back to Grand Cayman.

Luckily, the floors in my bedroom were hardwood, so there was no evidence left behind that I'd been pacing my room for an hour or longer early Friday night. Not like anyone was going to walk in while I ran around in circles in a bra and a jean skirt.

My parents insisted on taking Weezie for a sleepover, leaving me home alone in the tiny house I normally shared with my daughter. With my husband gone for good, I should stay put and concentrate on being the best mom I could be. Instead, I walked back and forth in front of my dresser, contemplating what to wear on top, or whether it would be best to just change into my jammies.

A romance novel called to me from the nightstand, and I paused my pacing, staring at it. I could make a cup of tea and crawl into bed for the night, no one the wiser. When Rylan asked why I didn't show up for the party, I'd blame it all on Weezie wanting me to stay home.

The windows were open, allowing a light breeze to filter in, along with the ever-present island humidity that threatened to return my just-straightened hair to salty natural curls.

Tony always said I was the quintessential beach beauty, whispering sweet nothings in my ear, trying to get me to agree to go out with him. He'd say my skin was perfectly bronze and my curls were perfect.

But none of his BS really mattered because I didn't care for him in that way. Tony was a project, and I'd already failed at a project like that. Ricky was my biggest failure.

Despite his compliments not swaying me to date him, Tony was a great guy. One of the best. Dedicated, loyal, and compassionate—he had all the character traits I should be looking for in a replacement father for Weezie. Only problem was Tony was a recovering alcoholic, and that scared me. Not to mention, he didn't do it for me. I always liked the bad boy . . . or the bad-for-me man, as in my current situation.

Blowing out a long breath, I pulled my mint-green satin tank top from the top drawer and slipped it over my head. The color did pop against my skin.

I shooed the thought from my mind because chasing the bad boy had already gotten me in trouble once, leaving me with an MIA husband and a daughter. Of course, Weezie was a wonderful bonus, but she deserved a dad. An involved dad, not an asshole who was off somewhere "discovering" himself.

*Discovering his dick is more like it.*

Freaking Ricky and his never-ending bellyaching over needing time to really know who he was, blaming my getting pregnant for his sad life, saddling him with a family and keeping him on this island.

*Whatever. I deserve to have fun too.*

At least, that's what I told myself as I ran my fingers through my hair and then applied a pale pink lip gloss. I slipped my feet into wedge sandals, my anklet with seashell charms tinkling with my every movement.

I'd admired the anklet every time I went over to the Grand, drooling over the expensive trinket sitting front and center in the display window of the overpriced jewelry store near the elevator. I made the mistake of stopping to look at it one day last year when I was delivering some coffee to the resort for my dad . . .

I'd been standing there staring at the gorgeous anklet in the window when a man came up behind me and whispered, "Beautiful."

Caught up in the moment, and maybe drowning a little in my own self-pity now that Ricky was gone, although I was the only one who knew it yet, I'd whispered, "It is."

We stood there for a while, the man's front nearly touching my back. He was so close, I could feel his breath on the nape of my neck, but I wasn't scared. Whoever he was, he radiated an aura of being in complete control. He seemed like the type of man who was always in charge of who, what, where, when, and why.

"It would look stunning on you," he said, sliding his palm down my arm and turning me to face him.

A man had never been so forward with me, taking such liberties in touching me without permission, and I never imagined myself to be the type who would allow it. When men got chummy with me at work, they got a tongue-lashing and the brush-off.

"I'm sorry," he said unapologetically. "I wanted to see your face."

I blinked at the gorgeous man in front of me, wondering what was happening to me. He was tall, with dark blond hair and yummy brown eyes, and a smile that I was sure had melted panties since he was sixteen.

He took a step back, putting some space between us, and said, "Cal," holding out his hand in introduction.

I stared at his large hand a beat or two before slipping mine in his. "Shell."

He smiled, and I nearly swooned. "Makes the bracelet even more appropriate."

Trying to pull myself together, I said, "It's an anklet, actually. My parents love this island, what can I say? I've lived here all my life. In fact, I'm delivering some coffee for my dad."

Holding up the bag to proudly display the family coffee shop's label, I sounded like a naive idiot who had never dated. Actually, I hadn't dated much. I got pregnant at nineteen.

"It's a beautiful island. By the way, I've seen that coffee before. My brother had some yesterday with his friend, Rylan. Must be a popular place."

"Ry? She's a good friend of my dad's. She was over at Camila's earlier in the week with a guy. Your brother, I'm guessing."

"Your guess is as good as mine."

The man ran his hand through his hair, and I noted flecks of gold dancing in his brown eyes, beckoning me.

Clearing my throat, I tried to think what I must look like to him, ultracasual in jean shorts and a pale pink tank top. At least my hair was down and smooth, not curly like it usually was.

"Ry doesn't really date, so probably. He seemed like a nice guy."

"He can be. I got dragged here for him, but it's not that bad of a place to get stuck. At least, what I've seen of it."

"Oh, did you—"

I never got to ask him if he'd seen a sunset on the beach here because a loud "There you are!" rang through the hallway.

A well-dressed, perfectly coiffed woman appeared, a small smile on her plastic-looking face, and slid her arm through Cal's.

"Sophia," she said to me boldly without waiting for an introduction, letting it be known she held a claim on this man.

*Territorial much?* I thought, then remembered my manners.

"Shell. I'm a local. I was just recommending a tour company. Don't forget, Sun and See Tours, with two e's." I said the last part to Cal in a hurry before scurrying off like a kid caught with both hands in the cookie jar.

Two days after I met Cal, my dad came by with a small gift-wrapped box that had been delivered to the coffee shop for me, but he didn't ask questions. He played downstairs with Weezie while I took it up to my bedroom, debating whether to open the box.

Once I opened the box and saw the pretty anklet I'd been drooling over, my eyes filled with tears. How could Ricky walk away from his family, and then a strange man be sending me jewelry, all in a few months?

The gift shouldn't make butterflies swarm in my stomach, but it sure did. I told myself to ignore those pesky little bugs, but I couldn't seem to take the anklet off.

Even worse, I'd never mentioned meeting Cal to Rylan, or about his coming back once to secretly check up on her for his brother. It had been shortly after that heavy-hitter guy nicknamed Chewy was here, and Cal showed up at Camila's.

Driven over in a car from the Ritz, Cal had explained that his brother was going through some things and missed his "secret vacation lover." Cal was here to see her from afar, so he could let his brother know she looked okay. He was staying at the Ritz, so he wasn't seen by anyone at the Grand or suspected of stalking.

I'd told Cal that he was kind of stalking, and we laughed.

Then his expression turned serious. "Actually, I volunteered for the assignment so I could see you."

One sentence, and I was floating on a raft in a quiet part of the ocean.

He stayed for dinner at a table for one in my section, patiently waiting for my delivery of his food and drinks all night. At the end of my shift, he insisted we have a glass of wine together.

And that was pretty much how the next five days went, his insisting I join him at the Ritz for a drink, or at the restaurant for brunch, or for a stroll through the shops in town. Each time, I gave in. I had to scramble for someone to watch Weezie at the last minute, but I did it anyway.

Cal didn't ask me much about Rylan, only said he'd caught a few glimpses of her and she looked fine. It was clear she hadn't moved on, and that was what he'd come to confirm for his brother. So, Cal decided to enjoy himself the rest of the time, and apparently that was with me.

One thing led to another, and I spent the night with him just before he had to leave. It was the only time I'd ever spend the night at the Ritz. The more I thought about it, I realized that maybe it was the only time I ever would . . .

Now, finally dressed and with guilt roughly the weight of an elephant weighing on me, I slipped out my front door to head over to Adam and Rylan's, berating myself once again for accepting the mysterious package delivered to the coffee shop that day.

# CHAPTER TWO

"**G**reat, you came!"

Rylan answered the door in a pair of cutoffs and a silky black tank. Her hair fell in waves down her back, and her feet were bare. She gave a whole new meaning to natural beauty.

In contrast, I found myself chewing on my lower lip, wondering if I was overdressed for the occasion in a jean skirt.

"You look fab," Rylan said softly as she pulled me in for a hug. Spinning me back out, she stared at me. "Something's different. Did you get a haircut?"

I shook my head, trying to ignore the frog that had taken up residence in my throat.

"I straightened it and then curled it," I finally said when I realized Rylan was waiting for an answer.

"I love it. You should do it always." Leaning close, she whispered, "You need to date."

At this point, everyone knew about Ricky leaving and openly scorned his decision. Once my mom decided she was done with my moping around, she told everyone she knew what a deadbeat he was. That was Marva, never one to mince words.

I gave Rylan a tight smile. "If it were up to my mom, I'd be walking down the aisle with one of her friends from church. She doesn't understand that will be a while. Two years with the way Ricky ran off."

"There's no rush to get married again," Rylan said, mirroring my sentiment. "But that doesn't mean you can't have hot sex." Her voice was whisper quiet beneath the music and voices floating from the other room. "You don't have to talk about Tony with me."

"I'm just trying to live my life, not get in my head, you know? Be there for Weez and manage some self-care."

Rylan squeezed my hand. "I got you. I was alone for a long time and liked it. Eventually, you'll find peace."

I nodded, trying not to blurt out that I'd already had one night of really hot sex with her boyfriend's brother.

"What can I get you to drink?" Rylan's question knocked me out of my naughty reverie. Rolling her eyes, she added, "Adam has Ben behind the bar. Offered him gobs of money."

"Well, that way you can have fun, Ry. You deserve a night off. I know for a fact you can't stay out of the bar area when you're at the hotel."

Tugging on my arm, she guided me toward the party. "Teddi should keep her mouth shut."

We walked through the foyer with Rylan's arm linked with mine until we got to the great room at the back of the house.

Like most people who lived and worked on the island, I knew the house used to be a pricey rental for expensive bachelor parties and family vacations. Adam bought it when planning to make his grand gesture and change his whole life for Rylan.

Now they both lived there, going back and forth to the United States for Adam's work and seeing his family. Except, his family was here now. Standing next to Adam was his brother, Cal, who was a little shorter, his skin lighter than Adam's olive.

Cal was no less attractive, though. With his own fair hair trimmed and wearing a gray polo, he stood with a drink in hand while talking with Adam. All I knew was the brothers were born as triplets but had lost their sister to tragedy.

"Hey, Shell, come on, let's get you a drink," Rylan said, oblivious to my foggy state.

Now standing in front of the bar area at the back end of the house, alongside the expansive windows, open to let the salt air flow in and out, I was only aware of Cal to the right of the bar.

"Hi, Ben," I said to Rylan's friend and coworker from the Grand Escape resort. He also loved Island Coffee and popped in regularly. We might have our secrets here on the island, but we all knew one another.

"Hey, Shell, you look great."

As Ben greeted me, the tiny hairs on the nape of my neck stood at attention. I sensed Cal's gaze land on me, and my body heated to what felt like two hundred degrees.

With my cheeks burning, I cleared my throat, attempting to play it cool. "Thanks, Ben. What are you mixing up?"

I knew Rylan, and there was no way she didn't come up with the menu herself—including the cocktails—to be sure the concoctions and combinations were perfect.

"Mojitos," he said, seemingly not noticing the man staring at me from the side of us.

I allowed myself a millisecond to glance at Cal before quickly turning back toward the bar. He'd been standing there, not even pretending to look at his brother, who was talking. Cal's eyes were fully focused on me. I knew they'd be the color of rich caramel, warm and melty, beckoning me to dive in and get stuck.

"Here you go." Ben slid a drink in front of me, and I wanted to chug it.

Instead, I took a sip, allowing the fresh lime-infused liquid to cool my throat, waiting for it to reach my belly and quench the fire raging there.

"Oh, I have to go check on the food." Rylan slipped away, the stacked bracelets on her arm tinkling as she hurried toward the kitchen.

Now that we were alone, Ben leaned over the bar and lowered his voice. "You doing okay?"

Like I said, everyone was mad at Ricky.

I nodded. "Yeah, it's nice to be out," I lied. The truth was, I wanted to run back home and put on my jammies.

"That's good. Hey, if you ever want to hang—" Ben didn't get the chance to finish because a deep voice interrupted.

"Shell." Cal said my name as if he owned it, his tone oozing with control and a hint of *step the hell back* directed toward Ben.

This was crazy. Cal and I had had one awkward moment outside a jewelry store and a few days of adventuring on the island. Of course, there was the one night. The best night of my life.

I had to bite back a smile that Cal had no idea that Ben was gay.

"How are you?" Cal's hand came to rest on top of mine, his palm burning through my hand on top of the bar. If Ben noticed the sexual tension, he didn't let on. He was busy helping a few guys line up shots.

"I'm . . . good. Yeah, good."

But I wasn't good. I was a bumbling idiot, absolutely nothing like the society woman who had sidled up next to Cal at the hotel, interrupting us when we first met.

"You never called or texted." His eyes bored into me, forcing me to remember what he'd said to me back then.

*You take the lead, and I will follow.*

Not meeting his intense gaze, I shrugged. "I've been busy. You know, with Weez and helping Dad."

Cal didn't respond, and the pause floated between us. One beat, two beats, three . . . until I couldn't take it anymore. Knowing he didn't believe me, I began to ramble like I did when I was off-kilter.

"It's just not a good time for me to start something with anyone, especially a long-distance thing because I have to think about my daughter, you know, because she misses her dad."

Cal leaned closer, never moving his hand. Nervous, I scanned the room to see if anyone was watching us, if anyone suspected anything. I hadn't mentioned knowing Cal to anyone.

"You mean her deadbeat dad?" he asked.

"Cal, don't. You don't know."

"I know enough," he said, his tone low and pure gravel.

Unfortunately, that growly voice did things to me I couldn't explain. I blamed getting knocked up at nineteen and not knowing a sexy come-on from a quickie on the beach, but if I were honest, I'd admit that Cal was different. Also, he wasn't the commitment type, no matter what he said. This I knew.

"I know enough too," I said quietly. "I know that this is a fun time for you, one that could leave me with a lifetime commitment."

"I see you're wearing the anklet."

*Typical Cal.* After only a few days spent together, I knew he was the king of redirection. I assumed this was what made him a successful divorce attorney. He could easily steer a discussion in whatever direction he wanted.

"We should probably separate," I said quickly, "and go mingle."

His hand tightened on mine, not in a painful way, but in a *no-fucking-way* way. "No reason. I've talked to a bunch of people who I didn't care about seeing, and now I'm seeing the one person who I wanted to see. I gotta say, it came as a surprise when Rylan said you were coming."

My throat felt like it was going to close. "You didn't tell her, did you? We—"

He shook his head. "Of course not. Neither did Adam."

"Oh, come on!" My voice rose to practically a shriek at the end. Quickly reining myself in, hoping no one had noticed, I said, "Adam knows? He's not going to keep secrets from Ry."

"He will when he doesn't want Rylan to know I was here spying on her."

Instead of giving him a useless rebuttal, I downed the rest of my mojito.

"Want another?" Cal leaned in a bit and inhaled near my hair while asking, as if I couldn't order my own drink. His voice even lower, he said, "You smell so fucking good."

Those words, meant only for me, hit me square in the chest, radiating warmth in my heart like I knew they shouldn't be doing.

"I'm driving later."

"I'll take you."

I scoffed. "And what, leave my car here? No thanks."

"I'll drive your car."

"Oh, you drive on the wrong side of the road now? Last I remember, you took a private car from the Ritz everywhere you went."

"I do. Well, I'm at the Grand now, thanks to Ry, but that ass did manage to set me up with a driver and car."

"What ass?"

"Tony, Rylan's bestie." Cal huffed out a breath. "I have to be nice, my brother tells me."

This was getting too complicated for me. The spiderweb of our connections was weaving itself tightly, strangling me. I couldn't decide if Cal knew Tony was pursuing me and mentioning him because of that, or if he simply didn't know.

Deciding to not dwell on Tony or call any more attention to him, I waved a hand in the air. "That doesn't explain how you'll drive my car."

Cal tilted his head, watching me. "Spent a semester of college in London. I can drive just fine on the wrong side of the road. Then I can call my driver to get me. Done and done."

"I'll stick with water for now."

"Weez at home?"

I hated how Cal shortened her name like I did. Even more, I hated how I'd allowed someone to know so much about my daughter.

Someone who would probably never meet her.

# CHAPTER THREE

"Hey, Cal," Rylan said as she strolled into the house, all pure happiness and good vibes. "I thought I'd see you at the hotel. Didn't they have your room ready yesterday?"

I was sitting in their kitchen, my ass firmly planted on a stool as I drank a sparkling water, wondering why the fuck I'd come back to the island. But I knew why.

Drawing a glass of water from the tap, Rylan continued to babble. "You could have stayed here. We have so much room, and we wouldn't have bothered you."

I shrugged. "No, it wasn't free yet, so I stayed at the Ritz. You know, houseguests are like fish, they start to smell after a day or two," I said, not wanting to reveal the real reason for my standoffishness.

"That doesn't apply to siblings, especially ones that shared the same womb."

"I think it's worse when siblings have shared the same womb. We want our own space, you know?"

"Cal, you don't have to put up those walls with me. I was an expert at it, and I promise you, it doesn't get you anywhere good."

Rylan studied me, her words a dagger to my heart. My brother had come here on a vacation to get over his own demons and fell for this young woman, twelve years his junior. He'd turned his life around because of her. For her.

"Yeah, yeah. I'm not putting up walls, Ry. I'm a grown man who likes his space."

"Whatever. You do you."

"I will. That's a promise," I told her, yet it was more of an affirmation for myself.

"Adam should be back soon," Rylan said, pulling me from my deep thoughts, or about as deep as they got.

"I know, he dropped me here. Went to get coffee beans."

She rolled her eyes. "The man loves his coffee, but he's also trying to talk Sam into expanding and letting Adam front him the money. Wants Sam to sell his beans to all the hotels in the area and on other islands."

"You don't say?"

There goes my fucking brother, wading in as usual. We had a few secrets even Rylan didn't know. Namely, I'd come to the island to have a private look at her when he'd gone back home. He wanted to make sure she hadn't moved on, and I'd wanted to be certain that hitting on wealthy tourists wasn't her MO.

I might have gotten myself tangled up with a local during that time, and while Adam wasn't happy about it, he wasn't going to tell anyone.

"You know Adam," Rylan said, "always the fixer. Shell's single now, and Sam wants her to join the family business officially rather than just working there part-time, but she won't. Adam thinks if Sam expands, then Shell won't be able to say no. Of course, Tony is opposed. He tolerates Adam but doesn't like him swooping in with a solution."

Glancing away, I said evenly, "I don't know anything about it."

Although I pretended to be indifferent to that bombshell, all the hairs on my neck stood at attention. I wasn't sure why Adam, Tony, or any Tom, Dick, or Harry had to be involved when it came to Shell. But I wasn't sure why.

All I knew was that it couldn't be me.

I didn't do long-term commitments, especially with single moms. My jam was beautiful women who liked me for my money and status. They knew the score, yet I couldn't get Shell out of my goddamn head.

I picked up my water, trying to cool my thoughts.

"Shell's waiting tables five or six nights a week, plus helping her dad and raising Weez. It's too much. Freaking Ricky."

There was nothing worse than a deadbeat. My mom raised us triplets on her own, but she had a sizable inheritance to keep her afloat. Shell had nothing, I knew, but of course I didn't share this with Rylan.

Nodding, I looked at my phone. "Look at that, my room is ready."

"You want me to take you, or do you want to wait for Adam?"

Standing, I put my glass in the sink. "Do you mind?"

Putting a big smile on her face, Rylan shook her head, probably as happy to get rid of me as I was to be leaving. "I have my Jeep. First time I've owned a car in . . . ever."

Ignoring her excitement, I wondered why I'd thought this trip was a good idea. I'd told Adam I'd slipped down to the island for some R&R, but I knew it was more about her.

*Shell.*

The one woman I didn't need to get involved with.

Now, as I stared at the beautiful bombshell, the rest of the room melted away.

Legs that seemed to go on forever were barely covered by her no-name jean skirt, and nothing but a skimpy green scrap of fabric hugged her breasts. As you'd expect, I'd dreamed about those breasts on lonely nights. I'm ashamed to admit that I'd longed for them on not-so-lonely nights too.

Yes, I was a dick of epic proportions. I had a great woman warming my bed in New York, but this woman standing in front of me, real and true, had stolen all my free thoughts.

Shell looked at me wide-eyed when I asked about her daughter, Weezie, as if she thought I'd forgotten she even had one. Shell's devotion to her daughter was the best part about her . . . and the worst. I had no business wading into this situation.

"Weez at home?" I asked again.

It was a trick question, and Shell would hate me for it. But not because I was a selfish man.

No, I wanted to hold her and cherish her body, make her forget she was a struggling single mom for one night. I'd give her pleasure until she couldn't take any more and collapsed in my arms with a smile. More than anything, I wanted to see if she'd known I was here, and had possibly decided to spend the night with me.

"She's with Mom and Dad. They like spoiling her."

I nodded, unable to take my eyes off Shell.

I'd been in a tailspin since Rylan had dropped the news that Shell would be at the party. Rylan had been inspecting my room at the Grand as she talked, making sure it was clean and perfect, and didn't notice that my world had tilted at her words. Rylan was like that, making sure everyone around her was comfortable and well taken care of, especially if they were staying at the Grand.

Still reeling a little, I told Shell, "Everyone deserves a little spoiling," and noticed her glance down at her ankle. "It still looks beautiful on you."

I made a mental note to stop at the jewelry store and see what else they had like that anklet.

"It wasn't necessary." Seeming nervous, she ran her palm over her arm, like a person searching for a lifeline.

Lowering my voice, I said, "I told you on my last visit, you deserved it. Let's move on and agree you're stunning, and you make that trinket sparkle more than it should."

Shell looked down as if staring at the stone floor, the pulse in her neck fluttering too many beats per minute.

"So, let's have a glass of wine and then I'll take your car home, and my driver will rescue me."

"Not your driver from the Grand."

I felt a growl coming up my chest. "Fuck him. I don't owe him an explanation." I meant Tony, but she didn't know that. "I hated having to do it, but my driver has been compensated to stay quiet."

"Premeditated, huh?" She glanced at me, and I loved her fire, how it shimmered just beneath the surface.

"I only heard a few hours ago you'd be here. I did my best."

I raised a hand in the air, drawing Ben away from another guest, and asked for two glasses of cabernet. When they arrived, I clinked my glass to Shell's.

"Go mingle. I'll find you later."

# CHAPTER FOUR

*Shell*

"Time to go," Cal said low in my ear after he'd made his way back to me. "Say your good-byes."

He walked away like he could boss me around, and I swallowed the notion that he could. Setting my long-empty wineglass on the bar, I looked around the room.

Ben was bent over under the bar, putting something away, and Rylan and Adam were nowhere to be seen. Probably in the kitchen micromanaging things, or outside with other guests.

I waved at Teddi, and she winked and blew me a kiss. She was cuddled in the corner, sharing a drink and conversation with a guy from the Jet Ski rental place. Of course, Adam had befriended the entire island in less than a month. They all knew him as the guy who had bought the big place in the West Bay.

Moving toward the kitchen, I found Rylan there, her head in the fridge.

"Thanks, Ry," I said, and she nearly jumped ten feet in the air.

"Shit, you scared me. I was looking for the half-and-half. Cal wants a cup of coffee." She jerked her thumb toward the coffeemaker brewing in the corner of the counter.

Frowning, I said, "I'm sure he could have made it himself."

*What is it with this man? Does he order everyone around?*

Rylan grinned at me. "Aw, thanks for thinking of me, but after a decade of serving drinks behind the bar, I always have coffee on when people are around. In fact, Adam used to slide behind the bar and serve himself coffee after we got back."

Her face took on a dreamy expression. She was such a goner for the guy.

"Well, you're the best," I said. "Thanks again for having me."

I needed to get the hell out of the kitchen before Cal came to retrieve his coffee. With half-and-half, apparently. I hadn't stayed long enough on the night I'd spent with him at the Ritz to know how he took his coffee.

"I'm glad you took time for you. You deserve it, Shell."

Rylan grabbed my hand and squeezed, almost as if she were trying to infuse me with her luck for falling in love. But there was no such thing when it came to me.

Speed-walking toward the front door, I decided to leave without saying good-bye to Adam, and hopefully before Cal knew I was gone.

The breath I'd been holding came whooshing from my mouth as soon as I crossed the threshold and made it outside to cross the long expanse of driveway to where I'd left my car, a used but reliable Mazda. I'd bought it with my tips. Ricky had scoffed at me, saying I could use the jitney or borrow my parents' car.

The guy was a dick, and I was dumb enough not to see it until it was too late.

Served me right for falling for the first guy to give me an orgasm, and it wasn't even an epic one. As time went on, I'd realized he didn't know his way around a woman's body. He'd just been the first man to touch mine—there.

"Hold up," a familiar deep voice called out as I slipped into my car.

*Shit.* I'd been caught up in my Ricky funk, and now I had to deal with Cal.

"Where are you going?" he asked, his voice low and rumbly, causing goose bumps to pop up all over my body.

"Home."

"The plan was for me to drive you."

I swallowed the lump in my throat, not from fear or regret, but apprehension.

Cal wasn't the kind of guy who committed to a woman or got attached, and I was just an inexperienced single mom. That was a bad combination, like fire and gasoline. My heart was combustible, and Cal was the type to run into burning buildings without a fireproof suit.

"I know," I said, "but it's for the best." I put the key in the ignition and tossed my purse into the passenger seat.

"I'm coming." Stubbornly, Cal stood there, blocking me from closing my door, and I felt myself nodding.

I wasn't going to lie . . . I wanted him to come and make me forget who I was for one night. My body itched for him to scratch it, like he'd done at the Ritz.

"I'll drive," he said.

Finally, my common sense returned. "No. Have your driver drop you at the café in town, and I'll pick you up there."

Cal pursed his lips, his eyes boring into mine. "Fine, but I'm not tiptoeing around that ass at the valet. He may like you, but you don't like him."

I pulled my gaze away from Cal. His directness hit me hard. I needed someone to speak to me truthfully, and no one ever did.

*No going back now.*

I slipped my hand into the interior handle and pulled the door closed. Cal watched every movement, including me putting my car into drive, and then he took off. To retrieve his coffee and find his driver, I supposed.

Stealing a glance at Weezie's booster seat in the back, I wondered if that would give Cal pause when I picked him up at the café. Maybe he'd change his mind and go back to the Grand and his New York society ladies.

"We could go to the Grand," Cal said as I pulled in front of my small house, and I tried to see my home through Cal's eyes.

Faded pink, in need of new shutters and a fresh coat of paint, it might not look like much to him. But it was everything to me.

Swallowing every ounce of my pride, I said, "I'm sorry."

"Why?" He half turned in the passenger seat.

"Because this can't be how you want to spend your vacation. In my crappy house."

He reached over the center console and stroked my cheek gently. "Is that what you think? That this is crappy?"

Unable to look at him, I stared at the console between us.

"Shell, look at me," he said, and I obeyed.

"This isn't crappy. It's you. In the city, they'd call it bohemian chic, but I call it all Shell. Warm and eclectic and welcoming . . . the same way I feel when I'm around you."

My heart skipped a few beats at his words. No one had ever said anything like that to me. I thought maybe it was me, but here was this gorgeous intelligent man saying it to me.

Staring at his eyelashes—they were way too long and perfect to be a man's—I smiled and leaned my cheek into his palm. "How do you know? We met in a hotel hallway, and then shared a night a few months later."

"I know," he said simply in his usual bossy way.

"Well, it can't be where you want to spend your time here."

The night sky was dark beyond the windshield, the ocean too far away to hear the waves, but the salty air rolled in through my open window.

"If you're here, then I do," he said, not giving me a chance to argue. "Come on. Let's go."

Cal pulled his hand from my cheek and was out of the passenger door before I could breathe. I felt my lungs gasping for air at his statement.

*Who is this man?*

He was the guy who had elicited a surprising reaction from me while spending time at the Grand with another woman. The same guy who had flew back to the island and swooped me up at the restaurant, then toured around the island with me for five incredible days.

And now he was outside my house, waiting for me to take him inside.

Blowing out a long breath, I opened the car door and accepted his waiting hand, then took him inside my house. The one my parents put a down payment on for Ricky and me. The house I'd paid the mortgage on for years because Ricky was always coming up short. The place where Weezie had learned to crawl and walk and talk, and then watched her dad leave.

"You know why I like this place?" Cal said as we walked inside. He turned around, taking it in under the dim light I'd left on. "It smells like you. Like fresh, sweet water. I can't explain it. They don't have that at the Grand."

Just like that, Cal dispelled any embarrassment I had about my house, and for the moment, any anxiety over inviting New York's biggest player home with me for the evening, or an hour.

By the time I'd laid my purse on the rattan chair next to the door and had kicked off my shoes, Cal was close, his breath ghosting over my skin. Mint and warmth swirled around me.

"Missed this," he said before kissing me.

My back hit the wall, and I was consumed by Cal.

At first, his kisses were slow and reserved, closed-mouthed but making me want more. Controlling the pace, he finally parted my lips with his tongue. I could feel my breath coming in pants, my chest heaving with desire.

"Open your eyes," he murmured into my mouth.

I wasn't even sure how he knew they were closed, he was so focused on devouring my mouth. When I obeyed, his knee moved up in between my legs and found my heat all too easily under my skirt.

My gaze met his, his searing through me, heating a fire like had never been lit.

His palm grazed my side, sliding up beneath my shirt, skin on skin now, sending tingles through my veins.

In one quick swoop, I was lifted into Cal's arms, my legs wrapping around his midsection of their own free will.

"Good girl," he told me.

I probably should have felt demeaned at his comment, but I didn't.

He pressed another kiss to my lips, then murmured against them, "Bedroom?"

One word, and I was pointing to the stairs.

He carried me up, the floorboards creaking under our weight. He found my room on the first try and set me on the bed, then toed off his shoes. Gathering my silky tank, he pulled it over my head, revealing my satin bra.

A hum came from deep in his chest before he told me, "Take it all off."

As I obliged, he joined me.

When we were left in nothing but our bare skin, Cal gently guided me back, shifting me up the bed. It was an intimate act, one I imagined was reserved for committed lovers, but it felt so right. Our nakedness felt like I was sharing my soul with him.

Surely, I'd regret this line of thinking in the morning, but at that moment, as Cal kissed his way down my body, I didn't care.

# CHAPTER FIVE

• **December** •

*Cal*

**M**erry *Christmas*, I texted back as I stepped out into the sun and looked for my driver.

I'd cooled shit off with Sophia back in October when I got back home from my last trip to the island, blaming work. For two months, I'd been putting off having "the talk" with her about our relationship.

Then she went and invited me to her parents' house for the holiday. Clearly, she wasn't getting where I was at with her, which was nowhere. I'd never promised her anything other than a good time, and I'd thought she was down with the program. Apparently, though, she was hanging on for dear life when it came to me. Yeah, we'd had chemistry in the beginning, but it had faded.

Waving, I signaled to Jack, the same driver I had the last time I stayed at the Grand. I could have rented a car, but I was a New Yorker these days. We didn't drive when we didn't have to.

"Hey. Welcome back," Jack said as he took my luggage and stowed it in the back of the Jeep.

"I see I've been downgraded from the town car," I said, slipping into the passenger seat. "No way I'm getting into the back of this thing. The wind will blow my ears out."

Jack nodded. "You asked for me, and this is the car Tony has me in this week."

*Of course. Tony.* I didn't say anything, though, because why breathe life into that jerk's name?

"This is more authentic, anyway. Happy holidays, Jack," I said, slipping him a few hundred-dollar bills as a holiday bonus, along with securing his continued discretion.

"Thanks." He grinned at me as he tucked the bills into his shirt pocket. "I'm saving up to get my girl some jewelry."

"Oh, you're at that point?"

"That's what she says."

We both laughed, and I wondered again how all these men settled for a lifetime with one woman. I'd never thought of myself as the type, but the peaceful feeling a certain island girl brought me made me wonder.

"Where to first?" Jack asked. "The hotel or your brother's?"

"I'm having Christmas Eve dinner at his house tonight, so the hotel. I do want to make a stop later before my brother's."

Jack nodded, knowing where I would want to stop.

We wound through some cruise traffic on the way to the resort where I'd reserved a villa through the thirtieth. If I stayed for New Year's by my lonesome, it was sure to send up some red flags. Everyone would be asking why I wasn't hitting up the New York club scene with a gorgeous woman on my arm for the ball drop at midnight.

When Jack pulled up in front of the valet stand, I told him I'd get my stuff and text him around four for my next stop.

Yanking my suitcase out of the back, I thought about the Lego set inside. Bribery was all it was. I'd never met Weezie, and I didn't plan on it. But I figured she'd be around for the holidays, and if I wanted to make nice with her mom, I'd have to pay the guard.

Laughing under my breath as I walked toward reception, I caught sight of Tony and Rylan out of the corner of my eye. She sent a wave my way, her watch reflecting the twinkly lights strung along the rafters. Bing Crosby floated in the air, and it felt wrong to be hearing "Little Drummer Boy" with no fresh snow outside.

For a moment, I missed home. Michigan, that is, where I'd grown up with my brother, and with my sister who was no longer with us. We didn't celebrate Christmas growing up. My mom would make us potato pancakes and give us candy coins for Hanukkah, but every year she'd take us to the mall to meet Santa. A result of us losing our father when we were little tykes, she wanted us to have someone to tell our wishes to.

"Hey, you made it," Rylan said, coming to stand next to me while I waited to check in.

Nodding, I said, "How's your friend? Is he behaving?"

She rolled her eyes. "Oh my God, even your brother has put the Tony thing to bed. What's it to you?"

"I'm the evil brother, I guess. If that dude wasn't nice to my flesh and blood, then I'm not sure about him. That's my job."

Although that's what I said, I was really asking because the ass had made a play for Shell. No way I was getting into that with Rylan, though.

Rylan nudged my elbow with hers. "Give it a rest, okay? So, dinner's at around seven. Adam was meeting with your client today over Zoom, and then he needed to run by Sam's to check on the holiday roast numbers."

"He's my hero, that guy of yours."

Rylan ran her hand through her blond waves and stared me down. As of tomorrow, she'd be my sister-in-law-to-be. She didn't know it yet, but I did. Adam had me look at twelve rings on FaceTime with him.

The whole process was nauseating, yet here I was to celebrate her holiday with the two of them. My brother said they had a menorah on the mantel, and Rylan was happily incorporating everything Jewish into her Christmas. Whatever that meant.

Luckily, the desk attendant waved me over.

"I'll be there. With bells on," I told Rylan and moved up.

She didn't bother to ask me to stay with them. I'd made it clear over the phone that I wouldn't. *Nope, I don't want to hear my brother banging you*, I'd told her, and she'd shut up.

Rylan was so easy to spook. She tried to be a hard-ass, but she was a romantic at heart. She was perfect in her new role as event planner at the Grand, coordinating weddings and engagement dinners when the sky was the limit at Grand Cayman's most exclusive property.

"Be nice, Cal," my brother's woman warned me as she walked away, and I knew why I was keeping this Shell thing from her.

I wasn't sure how much longer Adam would go along with it, but he had his secrets too.

"Stern for one," the receptionist said to me. "We have you in a two-bedroom villa with a direct ocean view."

The song had switched to some peppy version of "Feliz Navidad," and I wondered if this was the mood for the next week. A few women strolled babies through the lobby, and I hoped their rooms weren't near mine. I really was a Grinch, although a Jewish one.

"Here you go, Mr. Stern. Your room key. The number is written inside the folio. As you requested, the minibar is stocked, and a fruit plate has been sent up."

"Thank you," I said as I slid a fifty to the desk attendant. I wasn't sure if that's how they did things here, but in New York, we tipped.

"Oh, the bellman can leave my bag in the room," I told her. "I have to make a quick stop in the hotel first."

"Of course," she said, picking up the phone and asking the bell staff to come and retrieve my bag.

A young guy came over in a hurry and took my bag. The desk attendant whispered my room number to him, and he was off. I'd tip him later . . . I had an errand to run.

Legos, they had in New York, but the seashell jewelry was a local designer. I knew because I'd called the hotel's jewelry store and asked about the vendor. Touching the back pocket of my dark jeans, I made sure I had my wallet as I made my way down the hallway. Maybe I was only half a Grinch—I really wanted to get Shell something special for the holidays.

An all-too-eager brunette helped me select a pair of earrings, small hoops with an emerald-encrusted seashell dangling from each one. At my request, she quickly wrapped them, saying what a lucky woman would be on the receiving end of these.

Slipping my card back into my wallet, I hoped I'd be lucky enough to give them to her.

Shell didn't contact me between visits. I told her she could, and I always texted *good-bye* and *see you soon*, but our contact went no further. If I were being honest, this was uncharted territory for me. Usually, I was the one dodging texts and calls.

"Thank you," I told the brunette, whose name I failed to remember.

Another first for me. Beautiful women used to be my drug of choice. Without asking me, my body now currently only craved one woman.

"Here is fine," I told Jack. "Can you wait up the road?"

Jack nodded and gave me a two-finger salute.

He knew the drill. My whereabouts were my own business and no one else's. Luckily for me, I'd learned where Shell lived during my last visit. She hadn't wanted me to come in, but I'd insisted.

The pink clapboard house sat at the end of a quiet road. It wasn't much, with only two bedrooms, a living room, and a small kitchen and eating area. I pictured her sitting on the porch, having a glass of wine and relaxing like she deserved to do, but I didn't think she did that very often. The decor was an eclectic variety of styles, like Shell was a woman of various pursuits and passions.

Even armed with gifts, I knew it was a risk showing up unannounced, but this was how it went with Shell and me. We didn't talk, I showed up, we spent a few days together, and then we went back to our lives. If I were more of a man, I'd call or text and say I wanted to see her more, take care of her how she deserved, but the fear of rejection was strong with me.

I knocked on the door, hoping I remembered correctly when Shell said she always worked Christmas Eve night and her daughter spent the night with her parents. Like the stalker I was, I knew the restaurant always closed for a shift change between three and five.

"Cal?" Shell answered the door in jean cutoffs, and a white cable-knit sweater falling off her shoulder. She wore no makeup and her hair was in its natural curls.

"Merry Christmas," I simply said.

"Um, what are you doing here?" She stood in the doorway while I waited on the front porch, a box in each hand, looking and feeling like a stooge.

"I'm spending the holidays with Adam and Rylan."

"And you decided to just stop by unannounced. My daughter . . ." Shell raised a questioning eyebrow at me.

"Is with your parents. You said she always goes there on Christmas Eve to bake."

Hand on her hip, her head cocked to the side, Shell said, "And you were actually listening?"

"Yeah, I was listening. And before you tell me, I knew you'd be working later tonight, which is why I'm here now."

We stood there in a standoff, Shell staring at me, and me with no idea what to say. A definite red-letter day for a lawyer, let me tell you.

For a second, I thought I should have gone with Sophia to her family's house. With her, it was easy. She knew what I drank, where I liked to eat, and how I liked to fuck. Problem was, when it came to lighting a fire in my chest, she did nothing for me, nothing like how I felt with Shell.

This was the moment I confirmed I was twisted. Maybe not as twisted as my sister, who had battled mental illness throughout her too-short lifetime, but I was messed up.

Finally, Shell broke the silence. "I do have to work. *Soon.* Tonight is one of those nights we cater to tourists who want an island holiday. But do you want to come in?"

I nodded. "This is for Weezie." I handed Shell the gift wrapped in pink-striped paper with a red bow, no name attached. Something radiated between us as I said her daughter's name.

"You've never met her," Shell said, staring at the package with an odd look on her face.

"I know. I didn't want the holidays to pass and me be here without leaving something. From Santa, of course. It's Legos," I said, stumbling over my words, another rarity for me.

"She'll like that. Always wanting to create something, that one."

Shell set the package under the small tree adjacent to the front door. It was a short fake tree, decorated in popcorn strands and garland made of rings of red and green construction paper, twinkly lights twisted awkwardly around the spindly branches.

"Looks like she decorated the tree," I said.

"Yep."

Walking a step closer, I placed the smaller box in Shell's palm, then closed her fingers around it. "This is for you."

"You didn't have to." She stepped back, and I moved forward. "This is unexpected," she said, then swallowed hard.

I wanted to run my tongue down her neck and over her cleavage. I imagined yanking her sweater off and nipping at her nipple.

Closing my eyes, I bit back the savage in me. This wasn't the time for thoughts like that.

"Well, you didn't call or text . . . I knew you wouldn't, so here I am. Surprise."

Her chest rose and fell as her breaths increased, her slender shoulder peeking out from her sweater.

Shell's expression hardened. "We can't keep doing this. Weez is my life, and you have a great big world back in the States. We don't fit, Cal."

Her harsh words brought me back to reality. Never had I ever surprised someone for the holidays, gifts in hand. I'd never even dreamed of wanting to. Yet here I was in Shell's hallway, aiming for some grand gesture.

*We do fit*, I thought, but instead, I said, "You look beautiful. Go ahead, open it," I told her, gesturing to the box still in her hand.

She looked up at me, something undefinable in her dark eyes. "But I don't have anything for you."

"I don't need anything," I said, and I meant it. I earned all the money I needed and then some. "Actually, I needed to see you. So, you already gave me something."

I had no idea where this soft side of me was coming from, but it was alarming.

Without a word, Shell tore into the gift wrap and removed it from the box. As I watched, I realized I wanted her hands on me like that, removing my clothing to get to what was beneath. Thinking about how good it would feel for her palm to slide down my chest and over my stomach and further south, I watched as she removed the lid and took in the earrings.

"Oh," she said, lifting a hoop off the card that held it. "These are beautiful, but too much. I don't even have anywhere to where them."

"Wear them now," I said, pointing at her ear. "Let me see them on."

She shook her head. "The anklet was already enough. It's too much money."

Getting in her space, I said, "Let me worry about that."

"Divorce treating you well?" she asked, her tone snarky.

Standing toe-to-toe with Shell, I could feel her breath coming in angry spurts.

"I can't help that's what I do for a living. No matter which side of the table I'm on, I still try to advocate for the women and children to get what they deserve."

Shell let out a sigh and touched my arm. "Sorry, that was rude of me."

"I can help you, you know?"

She shook her head. "No. I could never afford your rates, and I don't want to owe Ricky anything. He doesn't deserve to even breathe Louise's name after walking out on her. He wants a clean break? Well, he can have one."

"I'm not going to bill you, Shell. For God's sake, I'm one of the best. People actually want to use me in their negotiations. If he wants to give up his family, he should pay."

"No, he doesn't want to give up anything. He just wants to be free, and I don't want to talk about this."

"Okay, so put the earrings on and offer me a drink." I didn't want to spend any of my precious time with her talking about the deadbeat anyway.

Shell brought the earring to her ear and slipped it into her naked lobe. I held the box while she finished putting on the first and then handed her the second.

"Gorgeous," I murmured. Unsure where this tenderness was coming from, I cleared my throat.

Shell gave me an apologetic look. "I don't have any booze to offer you. I wasn't expecting company. But I have a bottle of red."

"Good." Although I really wanted a Scotch to put out the fire of emotion in my throat, I said, "Let's have a glass."

I wandered to the kitchen, which was nothing like my gourmet one back home. I found a couple of wineglasses in the glass cabinet while Shell uncorked the bottle. For two people who were practically strangers, we navigated the tight space like seasoned lovers. That thought should have scared me, and it damn well did.

"Merry Christmas, Shell," I said as she poured the wine.

"Happy Hanukkah, Cal," she said back, highlighting yet another difference between us.

Skin color, age, religion, economic level, countries of residence—our differences were endless. Yet, standing here in Shell's imperfect beach shack, broken-down and in need of repairs, I felt perfectly at ease.

With all my tensions melting away, I downed a deep sip of wine and then set it aside. I took Shell's glass and set it next to mine, then brought my lips to hers. I gathered her close, my arm around her waist, holding her tight, giving her the support that no one else did. Then I kissed the fuck out of her like I'd wanted to for weeks.

Suddenly, some godawful noise started ringing through the kitchen.

"What the fuck is that?" I muttered as Shell whirled out of my arms.

"Work. My alarm. I thought maybe I'd catnap, so I set it," she said while turning it off.

"This is when you turn into a pumpkin?"

"I think you have the story mixed up. The carriage turns into a pumpkin, but Cinderella changes back to the working-class stepsister. And this woman right here has to go to work."

I kissed her again, wanting to shut up all her working-class bullshit. Not that it wasn't true, but in my mind, Shell was a goddess.

Why couldn't I tell her, though? Maybe that was a question for the shrinks.

"Can I see you later?" I asked when our lips broke apart.

"It's Christmas Eve, Cal. I have a daughter who will want to run home as soon as the sun comes up, so she can open her gifts and drink hot chocolate."

"Shit. Yes, of course." I shook my head slightly, annoyed with myself. "After the holiday? I'm here until the thirtieth."

"Of course you are. Who wouldn't want to be in New York when the ball drops?"

"You mean, home to start work in the New Year?" I said to correct her, even though she wasn't wrong.

"Right. I'll see what I can do. Weez is on break, so I'll see if my mom can watch her."

"Good. I'm off to Ry and Adam's for the holiday."

Shell smirked. "Don't tell them I said hi."

"Have the merriest Christmas," I said, ignoring her jab. Opening the front door to leave, I turned and added, "So crazy there's no snow."

Shell glanced at the blue sky. "I've never seen it."

Shaking my head, I wanted to say I'd show it to her, but thought better of it. We were secret fuck buddies, and it was probably best to leave things that way.

Our lives didn't fit.

# CHAPTER SIX

I have to take some beans to the Grand for Dad, I texted Cal. I'll come over (discreetly).

It was the day after Christmas, and of course my dad asked me to help out a while. My mom told Weezie she'd take her to the beach, and then make homemade mac and cheese with her. It was all part of their grand plan to get me to work full-time with my dad.

Cal had texted me late the night before to say Merry Christmas again, and that he wanted to see me. I didn't respond until now, and he immediately replied with *Room 156*.

He knew better than to pin me down for a time when I'd be there. I'd agreed to come, and that was about as good as it got with me with all my commitments.

Now, I quietly knocked on his door, wondering for a second if he was there, and then it swung open. Before I could utter a word, Cal snatched my arm and tugged me inside, shutting the door and pressing me against it, kissing me hard.

"Shell," he whispered against my lips.

"Cal," I whispered back.

"I love my name on your lips," he said, still whispering as he stepped back.

"Merry Christmas."

For a moment, I was lost in his eyes, brown with flecks of gold twinkling back at me, silently promising me a good time, a moment of respite from my everyday life.

Cal took another step back, and then I remembered I was upset with him.

Glaring at him, I propped a hand on my hip. "Did you forget to mention something?"

"Wasn't my news to tell," he said with a smirk. He ran a hand through his fair hair, a little long at the moment, curling at the ends. He had on a black polo and khaki shorts, no shoes, no jewelry except his heavy Rolex.

We stood a few inches apart, the last rays of daylight streaming through the billowing curtains, the smell of the sea filling the air, already heavy with desire.

I rolled my eyes. "Dad told me when I came in this morning. Of course, I called Rylan to confirm. She couldn't stop laughing about a Christmas engagement for the girl who never wanted to commit to anyone, but I thought it was kind of fitting. It's always the ones who don't want lasting love who seem to hit it just right."

Closing my eyes, I pushed away any further resentment toward my friend. Rylan didn't deserve it. After all, I had been the one who'd chosen Ricky, and I was the one who was now hanging out in a hotel room with New York's biggest playboy. My own choices had led to my current disappointment.

Cal grinned. "Well, she certainly seemed to bedazzle my brother. He's in it to win it with her. By the way, he didn't pop the question when I was there. Witnessing engagements isn't my jam. I couldn't get out of there fast enough."

There. He said it. Drew the line in the sand, so to speak. Cal was a good-time guy, and I deserved a good time. Period.

"That would have been awkward," I said, stating the obvious. "Ry texted me a pic of the ring, and it's so perfect. Of course, she says Adam is in a hurry to run down the aisle. I'll bet that the wedding will be sooner than later."

With a big honking three-carat emerald-cut diamond set among emeralds, a man who adored her, a new life in a huge mansion, and frequent travel, it all added up to a fast trip down the aisle.

Walking toward the bar, Cal said, "They're thinking of April."

"Oh, you would know." I stayed where I was, standing there like an idiot while my body tingled . . . for him.

"Adam told Ry that's how long she had. Until April, before summer and they traveled back to the States for a few months, and before the wedding season heated up for her work. He doesn't want to share her, he said. Drink?" Cal asked, changing gears just like that.

"Sure. Wine?"

He opened the mini-fridge and pulled out a chilled bottle of sauvignon blanc, which was what I liked best. I couldn't tell if he'd remembered that, or maybe it was just a lucky guess.

"I thought you might want some," he said.

*Ah. He remembered.*

He handed me a glass filled with a healthy pour, and then tipped a few fingers of Scotch into a tumbler. "Cheers."

Cal flicked a switch near the bar, and R&B flooded the room. Sade crooned, and I wondered if this was his act with all the ladies.

"I put in an order for the tasting menu. I just have to call when we want it brought over." It was then I noticed he had the table made up for dining, two candles flickering romantically in the center. When he noticed me glancing that way, he said, "They did it. Well, I asked, but the staff set it up like that. I can't take all the credit. I figured we'd be stuck in the room."

"Cal," I said before wetting my dry mouth with wine. "I can't go gallivanting all over the island with you again. I'm a mom with a daughter who needs me to be there for her, not floozing around. I'll look like the desperate spinster I'm destined to be."

For some reason, this made him laugh. He walked close, drink in hand.

"First, floozing? Is that a word?"

I nodded in response, a small smile turning up my lips.

Cal shook his head. "It's not. I went to law school, so I should know. I'd hardly call dinner and drinks at the Grand floozing if it were. Second, you're not a spinster, and definitely not desperate. If anyone is desperate, it's me. You have me panting for you, Shell. I'm happy to stay in, if that's how I get to spend time with you."

"Well, I'm glad you want me," I said. "I want you, but inside this room is all we have. A good time, and then we part ways."

It felt like I was reassuring myself more than him. At the same time, I didn't know where my boldness was coming from. This wasn't me, but maybe if I acknowledged our boundaries aloud, my heart would listen, so I went with it.

Cal nodded and took a swig of Scotch. I watched the sip travel down his throat, his Adam's apple allowing it to pass. It was as if I could feel the warmth spreading in his chest and belly.

"A good time it is," he said. "Have another sip, because then I'm taking your glass."

I did as I was told, and he did as he promised.

Our drinks finally resting on the end table next to the sofa, Cal guided me to the bedroom, where he took his time stripping me of my clothes.

First, he pulled my cream-colored sweater over my head, careful not to catch it in the hoop earrings he'd bought me. His palms caressed down my back and up again before he unlatched my bra, then swept in front and took hold of my breasts.

He worked wonders there, making my head fall back from the sensation alone, until he dropped to his knees and pulled my jeans down, followed by my red panties. I slipped my feet out of my clogs, and he yanked everything over my ankles, then ran his tongue down the length of my calf and up my inner thigh, to my most sensitive area.

I tried to watch, but inevitably, my head lolled back again as he found the bundle of nerves at my core. With his mouth, he brought me almost to the crescendo and then held me there for many breaths until I moaned his name and the word, "Please." It was only then that he let my world explode in front of my eyes. Once I'd had the orgasm to end all orgasms, he carried me to the bed, kicked off his shorts, put on a condom, and thrust inside me.

I knew there was a fiercer side of Cal he kept hidden. I wasn't sure how I knew—it was a feeling that came to me. He could be, would be, more assertive and even aggressive if I showed I was interested, but I didn't. The basics alone with him had me on the edge of falling too deep.

Assertive Cal might kill me. Not literally, but any chance of my heart surviving would be dead.

Afterward, we lay in each other's arms as if this was a normal everyday occurrence. Cal ordered our food, and room service discreetly served us a five-course meal while we were dressed in bathrobes. Later, we made love—I mean, had sex—again.

Before I sneaked out of his villa and drove home, I told Cal I didn't have coverage for Weezie the next few days, and wished him a happy New Year. He opened the door for me to leave, not pushing for more, and neither did I, for fear of getting too close.

Although, I doubted his reasons were the same as mine.

# CHAPTER SEVEN

• February •

*Shell*

I rolled over and into Cal's arms, not wanting to admit how much I'd craved the smell, touch, and feel of this man over the last couple of months since I saw him at Christmas.

Instead, I mumbled, "Coffee?"

Quickly brushing my hair away from my face so my curls no longer tickled my eyelashes, I quietly breathed in his scent. It was a mix of all man, coconut-scented soap from the hotel, and a faint hint of his cologne. Tom Ford, I knew, because I'd seen the bottle in the bathroom. I wasn't snooping, only lingering.

"I ordered it for seven. It should be here any minute," he murmured back, pulling me tighter into his arms and scent and invisible web.

"Oh, good. It's a new roast, an anniversary blend. That's what I was delivering yesterday when I sneaked in here. My sneaky deliveries are becoming a bad habit, you know?" I said, rambling like I sometimes did.

I wasn't nervous about being with Cal in this moment. Our carefully calculated nights where I was more stowaway than single mom had been the highlight of the last few months. If I was being honest, I was scared about what would happen when I wasn't able to steal these nights with him anymore. When he moved on, or decided I wasn't worth the trouble.

After all, wasn't that what Ricky had done?

Cal's lips grazed my temple, bringing me back to reality with his words. "Speaking of running the blend here . . . I want to know, are you quitting the restaurant?"

I shook my head where it lay against his chest. "No. I need the tips. It's important I do this my way. Don't worry about me."

"Your dad wants you to work with him full-time. Adam told me when we had lunch yesterday. Sam's putting pressure on Ad to talk with Rylan about it."

"Grrr," I said, sitting up and looking at Cal as I held the sheet to my chin, shielding my breasts from his gaze.

"Did you just growl?" His mouth formed a smirk, and I resisted the temptation to smack it off . . . or maybe kiss it off.

"No, I didn't growl. I said *grrr*. It's an expression."

"Is it now?"

The humorous moment made me pause as I took in beautifully handsome Cal. Soul-crushing Cal. Man-of-my-dreams Cal. He was a million fantasies and dreams wrapped up in one man.

His disheveled dark blond hair, eyes the shade of hazelnuts, long eyelashes any woman would die for, and small creases around his fortyish-year-old eyes spoke of life experiences I'd never have or even imagine.

"He wants you to have the time with Weez in the evenings, and thinks you deserve to work days. You're too old to work nights," Cal said, bringing us back to the conversation we'd been having.

We'd joked before about our sizable age difference—my twenty-six to his forty-one. It was only in these moments that I was hyperaware of how outlandish the two of us being together was, beyond the difference in our skin color.

"I wish you'd stay out of this with Adam," I said, trying to sound bossy.

Cal's palm came to my cheek and settled there. "He talks and I listen, babe. He said your dad wants it. It's the only reason your dad is letting Adam front the money for this project for him, so you can make a future with the shop. I can't help being involved."

"It's charity, Adam doing this with my dad. Then you get involved, and it cheapens what we have."

I blew out a long breath and lay back onto the pillow, the cool cotton enveloping me.

"I need to save for Weez. She's going to go to college and be something one day. That's up to me, not my dad or you or Adam. My parents don't get the part about my wanting her to leave the island someday. What would she do here . . . take over the family coffee shop? I don't want that for her. I want her to enjoy life, explore, live somewhere else."

This newfound independence and boldness I felt was deep in my gut. I needed to support my daughter, to encourage her to be better than me, and no one was going to stop me.

"Why?" Cal asked. "Her roots are here. And, by the way, this doesn't cheapen what we have."

He swallowed, and I shut my eyes for a beat.

"Cal," I said, placing my palm over his wrist, catching a quick glimpse of the contrast of our skin side by side. His golden-tanned white skin and my own was an unlikely blend. "We're having fun. I like this. I didn't want to admit it, but I do really like it. But let's be honest . . . this is nothing when it comes to the larger world."

"When I visit, it is what it is. But my life is in New York," Cal said, starting down his winding road of excuses.

I knew what the score was. We didn't need to speak it aloud.

"Shhh. It's enough. This is supposed to be my time away from all of those people and difficult decisions. We're the good-time crew," I said, letting Cal off easy because it was my turn to redraw the boundaries Cal had set.

He came to town, we had a good time, and then he left. We didn't get serious or worry about each other, and I didn't contact him in between.

And this worked. No one knew about us except Adam, who had kept his word to be discreet. Our time together was like this tiny island of privacy and excitement I held close, just for myself.

"Come sit outside on the patio. No one is going to walk by. It's seven in the morning," Cal said when he came back to bed with the coffee tray. "It's gorgeous out," he added while tilting his head toward the window.

The one thing the Grand Escape prided itself on was privacy. Flowers and shrubs surrounded the patios of the villas, giving guests privacy, while the sounds of the ocean filled the air around them.

I nodded, snatching a robe off the floor and slipping it on, then cinching it tightly around my waist as Cal poured two coffees, adding half-and-half to his and leaving mine black.

Like a couple who did this often, I held the door open to the patio and he walked past, coffees in hand.

"Your witch's brew," he said, handing me mine.

"A mom needs all the strength she can get."

Cal sat next to me in a pair of athletic shorts, no shirt, his firm chest on display, and took a sip. "This blend is good." Just when I thought he was skillfully sidestepping any mention of my mom life, he said, "You know I get that, moms needing strength. My mom raised the three of us on her own."

I nodded, knowing the story from Adam and Cal. Their dad died when they were toddlers, leaving their mom alone with triplets.

"Adam was our caretaker. He seemed to take my dad's absence the hardest. I guess that's why he struggled so much when Becca took her own life. It's not that I didn't feel it in my gut. Every time I think about her, it crushes me. But Becca was Becca, and she struggled. We all did our best to help."

Cal had never talked about his pain this way. When I looked at him, it was as if he wasn't real. Rich, good-looking, always up for a good time. Seeing this side of him made me look at him in a new light.

"I think it's why I want to live so hard," he said. "To suck the life out of every moment. For Becca. Since she can't do it, I want to do it for both of us."

I nodded again, unsure what to say. I had no idea what he really meant. I was struggling just to survive, barely able to enjoy these fleeting moments between us.

"Anyway, enough talk about all that." He took another swig of coffee. "My view is too gorgeous to get caught up in life's tragedies."

When I looked up, his gaze wasn't on the flora or the ocean in the horizon. It was on me.

I dropped my gaze to my coffee, needing to catch my breath. When I tried to look back at him, but I couldn't. It was in these moments I knew better than to show my inner feelings.

"If you could, I'd have you tell your dad how great this is," he said, holding up his cup. "You know, I don't mind you saying anything."

Horrified, I shook my head. "I can't. You know this. It just wouldn't be right for my parents to know. Their heads would fill up with ideas about us, about a future, and this is . . . well, it is what it is."

We'd had the conversation once before. Back in June when I'd first spent the night with him at the Ritz . . .

I had been lying in bed, twisted up in the sheets, satisfied in a way I'd never been before.

Cal had moved up in the bed. Taking me in his arms, he whispered, "I like this." He held me a bit tighter, so my head rested on his shoulder. "I could come back anytime. Or you could take a break and come see me."

I shook my head as my heart pounded hard, begging me to say yes. Instead, I'd asked about the woman he was here with last time.

"We have a good time together," he said, kissing the top of my head. "But I like this."

I didn't know what any of it meant or how to handle it. I was a naive single mother, with little to no relationship experience other than a failed marriage.

Realizing I was in over my head, I'd said, "This is a good time between us, but that's it. No one can know, and it can't be anything more than this . . ."

Since then, I'd become Cal's vacation booty call, and was happy enough with that. It was all I could expect from him, or give to him. I'd never asked about the society woman again, but I was certain that if she weren't still around, another woman just like her was in her place.

"And what is it?" Cal narrowed his eyes, parroting my words back at me.

"You know, a fun time?"

He blinked, then nodded. "Doesn't mean we can't have fun more often."

It was then it dawned on me, he didn't mean more of a relationship. He meant more booty calls.

I almost burst out laughing, but stopped myself. Afraid I'd lose the tiny piece of Cal I had, I swallowed my chuckle. "This is as much as I can give."

He took my empty cup and set it down on the table, then hoisted me onto his lap. As I straddled him, he ran his fingers through my hair. "I'll take it. Whatever you're giving."

And there, in the most beautiful place on earth, surrounded by luxury I'd never be able to afford myself, he started kissing me, and I fell deep in the moment. My head rang with the word *dummy*, but my heart soared like a dolphin leaping out of the ocean.

Pulling back, he said, "Dinner tonight?"

"I have to see if my mom will take Weez again. She probably will. They adore her more than me."

"Impossible."

"Enough with the compliments," I said, then kissed Cal again to shut him up.

Much later, after he brought me to orgasm with his mouth and had his way with me in the shower, he said he was going to golf with Adam.

"Chewy is here. Can you believe that guy? He's looking at buying a vacation house here, near Adam. Dude is flat-out obsessed with my brother since Adam found him a few extra mil in his divorce."

"And Ry planned his wedding," I said.

"That too."

Dressed now, I checked myself in the mirror. "Gotta go." I had to work lunch at Camila's before picking up Weezie from school.

"Come anytime later. Text me. I can have them cook whatever we want and send it to the room. A belated Valentine's dinner," Cal said with a wink.

I rolled my eyes. We didn't do Hallmark holidays. Valentine's Day was over ten days ago. I knew because I'd celebrated over pink-iced cupcakes with Weezie, and then gone to bed alone.

As I left the hotel the back way, I mentally slapped myself.

*What am I doing?*

Cal had the world at his beck and call, and I was heading out to wait tables for tips so I could send my daughter to college one day. These moments were nothing but slumming for him, but they were a dream come true for me.

# CHAPTER EIGHT

• April •

*Shell*

My skin was burning hot, and it had absolutely nothing to do with the bright sun above Weezie and me at the Grand's pool.

My temper flared, and my pulse raged, pounding in my ears as I tried not to clench my hands into fists. I told myself to breathe as I stared at the two of them from afar.

For some reason, I was shocked, when I had to have known somewhere deep inside this was going to happen. After all, this was Cal. The man did what he wanted, when he wanted, and how he wanted. He showed up when he felt like it, and went back home before he was ready in order to protect himself. He was allergic to commitment and afraid of his feelings.

I knew this. He knew this.

Yet, seeing him here on the island with the bitchy woman from so long ago cut deep. I had to wonder . . . had he been seeing her all this time? He'd mentioned being single and not involved with anyone, but this was Cal.

"Mommy, can I get in the pool yet?" Weezie whined from the lounge chair next to me, interrupting my trip to a personal and private hell.

I never should have accepted Rylan's invitation to spend the day at the pool at the Grand, but Weezie had been dying for a vacation. This was about as close as she would get, especially since I'd insisted on doing things my way, waitressing for tips rather than working for my dad.

Soon, though, I'd be unable to do either.

"Two more minutes," I told Weezie, looking at my watch. She'd just polished off a basket of chicken fingers and fries Rylan had sent over with a Shirley Temple.

I licked my thumb and used it to rub a little ketchup off the corner of my daughter's mouth. She only squirmed a little and then settled down until I was satisfied her face was clean.

"Can I go in the deep end?" she asked, and when I didn't say anything, she added, "Please? I've been waiting, Mom."

"When I say so, and then I need to go with you."

Of course, I wasn't showing yet, but my stomach had widened, and I still had a tiny pooch left over from Weezie, so I looked the same as always—like an overworked, tired, single mom. The last thing I wanted to do was stand up in my bathing suit in front of him *and her*. Sophia, the perfect New York lady. She probably sunbathed nude outside their villa, and had zero stretchmarks to hide or fucks to give.

I knew my body wasn't completely disgusting. After all, I did my best to keep myself together, and obviously Cal liked what he saw enough to knock me up.

"Is it two minutes?" Leave it to my daughter to try to hurry me up.

"It is, sweetie. Let's put on a little sunscreen, and we'll go."

She popped up, closed her eyes, and stood in front of me for me to apply the lotion to her skin. Thanks to Ricky, her skin was lighter than mine, but her perfect nose and headful of dark curls were all mine.

I couldn't resist placing a quick kiss on her check and tapping her tush. "Let's roll, baby girl."

Like a rocket, Weezie was off and running toward the deep end, leaving me little time to jump up and follow her. At least I didn't have time to agonize over Sophia, because now I had to worry about my daughter drowning. As Weezie pinched her nose and jumped in, feet first, I tried not to think about how I'd gone and gotten myself pregnant for the second time without being married.

I picked up my pace when I saw a fully dressed Cal jump up from his seat and dive into the pool in slow motion. Weezie's head broke the surface and she tread water as best she could, dogpaddling to the side before Cal swooped up from below, capturing her in his arms.

I was at the side of the pool as he said, "You okay, tiny mogwai?"

Weezie wrapped her arms around Cal's neck and nodded at him, her eyes wide and sparkling.

*Yeah, I get it, baby girl.*

With my daughter in his arms, Cal kicked toward the side as she asked him what a mogwai was. He plopped her on the side of the pool, her wet tush making a puddle underneath her.

"I think you lost something," he said to me before lifting himself out of the pool in soaked khaki shorts and a polo. I swore I could see his eyes dancing behind his mirrored shades.

"Thank you. She was okay. I was on my way." The fragments rolled from my mouth as Cal stood up next to me, dripping water everywhere.

"I wasn't sure if any little kids should be jumping in the deep end like that," he said.

Of course he wasn't. Cal was a confirmed bachelor. He'd never met Weezie, had no idea she was taking swimming lessons, and there was a reason for that. Kids craved attachments, and Cal avoided them.

I'd wanted to call Cal every day for the last two weeks to tell him I was pregnant, but I chickened out, partly because I'd never called him between visits before. The other reason was this—Caleb Stern wasn't made to be a father. Knowing he was coming to his brother's wedding, I'd decided it was a better idea to wait and give him the news in person.

That was all before I knew he was bringing Sophia to Rylan's wedding. Maybe if I hadn't been lying to Rylan about my relationship (or lack of one) with Cal, I could have asked her for her opinion. And now I'd gone and made myself an awfully messy bed to lie in.

"What's a mogwai?" Weezie hopped to her feet, yanking on Cal's soaking-wet polo. He didn't know she was a dog with a bone when she wanted to know something.

Surprising me, he knelt down. "A mogwai is a tiny critter that if it doesn't go to bed on time, it turns into a wild and furry creature who does naughty things."

"Am I bad?" Weezie asked, looking to this strange man for confirmation. A man I knew intimately, yet she'd never met. It wasn't like he meant anything to her, but since Ricky abandoned us, she'd been seeking the approval of every man we came into contact with at school, the restaurant, and now, apparently, here.

"No, you're not. Your mom wasn't worried about you . . . I was. That's all."

Weezie nodded. "I'm learning how to swim at the community center, but my mom works nights, so my *abuelo* takes me, and he gets nervous too."

Glancing to the side, I noticed Sophisticated Sophia was watching the whole scene unfold from a chair at the bar, sipping a Pellegrino, no doubt. Not like she would have jumped in to save my daughter.

Cal stood and brushed Weezie's wet hair from her eyes. "That's your grandfather's job, to be nervous. Sounds like he's doing it well." Giving me a quick scan, he murmured, "Nice anklet."

*Oh no.* A man like him couldn't know that kids home in on a murmur more than the normal speaking voice.

"It was a special, special gift from a guardian angel," Weezie blurted just as Sophia decided to grace us with her presence.

Taking a quick look at my daughter before sliding her gaze to me, she said, "You're the girl who works here, shlepping coffee, right?"

I wanted to shrivel up and die, but refused to let my daughter see me cower. Reminding myself that I was a proud, working single mom, I lifted my chin. "Yes, we met. And my dad owns that coffee shop and beanery. He supplies the hotel, and I was making a delivery for him."

Ignoring what I'd said, Sophia went right for the jugular. "So, are you staying here?"

When her nose turned up in the air, I changed my mind. She wasn't Sophisticated Sophia at all. More like Snobby Sophia or Shitty Sophia.

"No," I said with a very tight, very fake smile. "We're just here for the day."

"Yeah, Rylan invited me to swim and have a Shirley drink," Weezie said helpfully.

Sophia raised a brow, gesturing between my daughter and me. "You know Rylan."

"Yes," I said with a nod.

"Oh, I thought you were helping a stranger," she said to Cal. "But you know this girl and her child. Rylan will be happy. Maybe that will win us some points with your mom. She was certainly surprised to see me here."

I had no clue what all this meant, and I didn't care.

"Sorry you got all wet on our account," I said to Cal. "Thanks for helping Louise."

I didn't want to use her nickname in front of Sophia. I didn't want this woman anywhere near me, my child, or my feelings.

The only problem was . . . somehow I had to tell her boyfriend over the next few days that I was pregnant with his baby.

# CHAPTER NINE

*Cal*

"Thanks, Theodora," my brother said to a gorgeous redheaded bartender who rolled her eyes at him.

Last year, I'd have asked her for her number, but now I was officially fucked in the head. Seriously fucked.

With two tumblers of Scotch in front of us, Adam said, "Cheers. I think that's what you're supposed to be wishing me. I'm the one getting married at the end of the week."

I took a swig of my beverage, needing to feel the burn down my throat. Once the Scotch had done its thing, I growled out, "*Mazel tov*," deciding to go with a mix of sarcasm and Jewish sentiment.

My brother eyed me, his blue eyes inspecting my brown ones, looking for some insight into my grumpy mood. Admittedly, it was unfair of me to act this way, but Adam and I were born of the same womb, so I took liberties when it came to him.

"Mom is arriving in the morning," he said. "Is that what has your boxers in a bunch? Rylan better not catch wind of you acting like an ass. This is her week, and I don't want anyone or anything to upset her. She's had enough of that with her parents, who aren't coming to the wedding and don't deserve her second thought."

We sat in the lobby bar of the Grand, a place I'd come to think of as my home away from home, probably due more to one particular island inhabitant. And here I was thinking of Shell, rather than my wedding date, who was showering and getting ready in my villa at this very moment.

Like I said, I was fucked in the head.

I was obsessed with a woman who lived on Grand Cayman. A single mom who lived a simple life, and I was a hard-charging, hard-partying New York lawyer. To say we were opposites was an understatement, which was why I bit when Sophia said she wanted to come to the wedding. Sophia was the type of woman I should be with.

"Mom is fine. She'll be carrying on about my date, saying I should marry a nice young Jewish girl in New York and have a family, move to the burbs, buy a dog, go to temple," I said to my brother, stating the obvious.

"*Jewish* girl," Adam said. "You know she won't care when it comes to finally settling down."

"Please. You get to have the woman of your dreams, and me, I have to live out Mom's dreams."

Adam took another swig of his drink. "Is that why you brought Sophia, to make a point to Mom? To let her know you're not going to play by her rules? I thought you and Sophia were done around Christmas, and you've been back here since to see Shell."

"Quiet," I growled low. "This place has ears, I swear."

I eyed the redhead. She was friends with Rylan, so I assumed she knew Shell, and I didn't need Shell's name even breathed at the bar.

"Look, Adam, I've seen Sophia a few times—as friends and trying to shake her off—since being back home. It's not serious, but she saw the invite and said she was there when you two met and insisted I bring her. She was convincing, and I figured some companionship would be good because I can't keep coming to see you-know-who. It's not going to work."

Adam set down his drink, taking a moment before speaking. "Cal, I'm just going to say this. It's time to stop sleeping with two women at the same time, even if they live in different countries. You can't play games like that."

This made me laugh. "You're kidding, right, lecturing me? Well, I'll have you know the boundaries have been set with Sophia. At first, she didn't want to sleep with me after the holiday fiasco and my turning down her offer to meet her family. I let her have that because I don't want to sleep with her. I don't even know if"—I lowered my voice—"I could get it up with her."

Sitting back in my chair, I stared at the dumbfounded look on my brother's face.

"Why, you ask?" I said, not giving him a chance to speak. "Because I'm fucked in the head. Now, I told her I want to slow things down. Sophia, I mean. She suspects something's up, but at the end of the day, all she cares about is saying she's with me. This is less effort."

"Cal, Cal," my brother murmured, shaking his head in disapproval.

When we both finished our Scotch, Adam motioned to the bartender for another round.

Glancing at me, he said, "I need it after that little monologue from you. Shit. You need help."

I didn't have time to respond because the redhead decided to interrupt in this moment.

"Heard you jumped in the pool today fully clothed," she said conversationally like we were besties. I'd seen her at the hotel before but hadn't chatted much with her.

"What?" Now fully invested in yet another fiasco of mine, Adam swung his gaze to me. "Your date force you to drink too much on the flight?"

Not meeting his eyes, I shrugged. "No. It was nothing."

The redhead shook her head. "It was the talk of the break room. I was glad Ry was off today dealing with her dress or lack thereof. The girl is anti-wedding, but that's a conversation for another day. I heard you jumped in to save a kid."

Waving her off, I said, "The kid was fine. I made a bad call."

"What kid? You and a kid?" Adam leaned closer, now on a deep-sea fishing trip when it came to the details.

"Shell's kid," the redhead said. "Weez."

It was then I was reminded how Shell had called her Louise at the pool, denying me any familiarity. Seeing Sophia with me must have been a gut punch, and Shell had every right to be mad. I had no idea she'd be by the pool today.

Adam's gaze slid to me, and he raised an eyebrow but didn't say a word.

I turned to look at the bartender. "I'm Cal, by the way."

"I know. I'm Teddi. I've seen you coming and going lately. A lot," she said, sporting a smirk.

Was it my imagination, or did she know more than she was letting on?

"The kid was fine," I said, "but I thought she couldn't swim."

"And you jumped in to save her?" Adam asked. "Weezie?" he said incredulously, eyeing me like I was an alien life form.

"Yeah."

"Is she okay? Sam's going to be upset if anything happened to her. He babies her."

I drew in a breath through my nose. "Look, I already said she was fine." Teddi stood within earshot, so I added, "And I apologized to her mom for doubting the kid's swimming ability. I'm not a bad guy."

Adam nodded at me with his brow scrunched before he took another sip of his drink, then leaned in again. "It's my wedding week, Cal," he said, dead serious now. Lowering his voice to a whisper, he added, "Don't fuck this up."

I knew he meant it. If I messed anything up with Rylan or this wedding, he would kill me. Slowly.

"Hey," a voice with an uppity New York accent said, interrupting the moment.

I looked up and found Sophia standing there, her hair unusually poker straight and with a full face of makeup. She was wearing a black minidress that was way too tight.

"We're eating outside," I said, taking in her look, which screamed *New York VIP club*, rather than *casual Caribbean outdoor dinner*.

Staring at me, she said, "I just spent an hour straightening my hair, Caleb. Outside isn't good for it."

It took everything I had not to roll my eyes.

Adam stood and smiled. "Hey, Sophia. Good to see you. I have to meet Rylan over at Camila's, so I'll catch you later."

He put special emphasis on Camila's, and I swore Teddi looked up.

"Oh, okay. What's Camila's? Are we going there?" Sophia asked both Adam and me.

"It's a local place. More beach shack than Michelin," Adam said with a knowing smirk.

"Never mind. Like I mentioned, my hair," she said, flicking aforementioned hair over her shoulder. "Maybe we can eat somewhere else? Here, maybe?"

Adam sneaked off, leaving us alone. He was probably afraid he'd say more than he should.

"We're in the Caribbean," I said. "We're not doing Camila's, but Rylan recommended a place over by them in the West Bay. It has outdoor seating and is on the water."

Sophia waved her hand in the air at Teddi, acting like the bartender was her own personal servant, and bile crawled up my throat. "Glass of pinot noir," Sophia said to a scowling Teddi, no *please* or *thank you*.

Bringing Sophia to the wedding was a mistake . . . a huge one. I didn't usually make errors like this. Typically, I was a very calculated man.

Holding my breath, I watched as Teddi eyed her and poured the drink without flinching, but this girl was hip to more than she was letting on.

"Here you go," she said as she slid the wineglass toward Sophia on a napkin.

Not missing a beat, Sophia picked up the glass and took a sip without a word of thanks. To me, she said, "It's fine. I'll see if the hair salon here can take me tomorrow and before the wedding, so I don't have to keep wasting my time."

Her dark eyes on me, Sophia waited for me to respond, knowing that the salon charge would go to the room and be paid by me, so I nodded. Sliding into the chair Adam vacated, she sipped her wine.

"I don't know why we can't hire a town car," Sophia said, continuing to whine. "The Jeep is so bumpy."

Wow, I was really regretting my poor choices when it came to her. But here we were, so I needed to try to make the best of it.

"I thought it would be fun," I said, forcing a smile. "I'm brushing up on my wrong-side-of-the-road driving skills now that Adam lives here."

*And Shell lives here* sneaked into my thoughts before I could stop it. Like I mentioned, I was fucked.

Taking a deep breath before Sophia could respond, I said, "Shall we?" I knew Sophia wouldn't finish her wine. Too many calories, so she would be happy to be done.

"I'm going to check with the concierge on hair appointments," she said and left me to handle the bill.

I looked at Teddi, who was busy cutting a few lemons in the corner, and she popped over.

"Something else?" she asked in a saccharine tone that I knew was purposeful.

"Just the check."

Teddi reached for it and slid it over to me. "She seems like a nice gal."

I looked up from signing the check with my room number. "You always provide this type of commentary to customers?"

"Nah, just the special ones," she said with some sass.

"Well, she's not a nice gal. I'm starting to realize that."

Teddi raised a brow. "Just now?" She poured me an extra finger of Scotch. "On me. You may need it, and maybe you should take that driver. *Jack.*"

I slapped a fifty-dollar bill on the bar. "From me, and I think I may do just that if it will get her to shut up and allow me to drink some more. I don't think driving is in my future this evening if I want to stay sane," I said, humoring the bartender.

I wasn't going to bite on her comment about Jack, though. She was obviously baiting me.

"Want me to call out to the valet and see if Jack's free?"

Downing my Scotch, I said, "I have his cell."

"I thought so. For all those secret outings."

"Didn't we just meet?"

Teddi nodded. "But I feel like I know you, plus you seem like a decent guy, saving Shell's kid."

"I didn't save her. She was fine."

"Who will save Shell?" Teddi said, giving me the eye.

"Christ," I murmured. "I don't know what you're getting at, but you need to cut your fishing expedition short." I stood without waiting for her reply. "Nice meeting you."

Did Shell tell Teddi? Or did everyone on the island know about us?

As I texted Jack, I imagined the hairdresser telling Sophia about Shell.

*Fucked* wasn't a strong enough word.

# CHAPTER TEN

*Shell*

I t had been three long days since I'd seen Cal. I'd made myself scarce around the coffee shop and the restaurant—both places he'd look for me if he weren't here with another woman.

I avoided the resort as if it were a plague. Every morning, I'd text Rylan and ask if she had any wedding-related tasks for me, and she willingly sent me on odd errands.

*Pick up some Jewish marriage contract at the airport, grab embroidered head coverings that Shanna, the local seamstress, had knit for her, and talk to Dad about his outfit.*

I was happy to do it all because it kept me busy and out of sight of the wedding party.

When I found myself with some downtime, I googled Jewish weddings, curious about what I was picking up and what the men were wearing on their heads. All Rylan cared about was a wedding without formalities and meaningless gestures, and all Adam's mom wanted was a traditional Jewish wedding—so Rylan was having both.

"Hi, Dad," I said, walking into my parents' house on the eve of the wedding.

"Shell, where have you been? I waited for you to swing by the shop today to deliver the beans for the wedding. I ran them over myself."

"Oh, I had to go get yarmulkes. You have to wear one."

My dad waved a dismissive hand. "I know. I had a Jewish friend growing up."

"You did?"

"I'll explain another time," he said. "Your mom is upstairs hemming Weezie's dress."

"Did you finalize your clothes? Ry doesn't want you in a suit."

My dad, who I'm sure looked forward to putting on his Sunday best, nodded. "Navy pants, white shirt, yarmulke, underwear. I told Adam today when he stopped in."

"Oh. Well, I guess he didn't tell Rylan yet."

Dad stirred some sugar into an iced tea. "His brother was with him. Kept asking me about you, about if you were going to work with me. Blamed it on Adam bothering him, but I didn't like it. What's it to him? He lives in New York."

I shrugged. "Who knows? He's a stiff one. Probably worried Adam is making a bad investment."

"That the brother who saved Weez?"

I tried not to roll my eyes. I was so sick of everyone knowing and asking about the near-drowning incident, which wasn't so near drowning.

"Yeah, Adam only has one brother. You know that, Dad. Did you mention it?"

"Well, he didn't seem like the type to do that type of thing when I saw him today, so I didn't. He seemed like a jerk."

I found myself wanting to defend Cal, which was absurd. Thankfully, Weezie appeared in her bridesmaid dress.

"Mommy, look," she sang while spinning, the tulle skirt swishing around her.

"Gorgeous, baby girl." I took in the wondrous creature before me and wondered if my heart would grow enough to love another as much.

"You look flushed," my mom said as she entered the kitchen, looking me up and down. Then her gaze paused on my middle and her eyes narrowed.

In this moment, I knew she knew, and we shared a quiet exchange. She squinted her *Catholic knowing I sinned eyes* at me, and I lightly shook my *don't say anything head* at her.

"Why don't you go get some rest?" Mom said, not waiting for me to respond. "We'll take Weez for dinner, and maybe she'll stay over."

"You don't have to," I said, because the last thing I wanted was to be alone with my thoughts.

Cal was probably running around the island with Sophia, eating, drinking, and being merry. She might not be Jewish, but she wasn't a local islander with brown skin and a child. I imagined Cal and Adam's mom wanted a Jewish life for both of her sons . . . not only Adam.

Weezie begged, interrupting my thoughts. "Mom, please!"

"Okay, baby. But the wedding is tomorrow, so make sure to go to sleep when *Abuela* tells you."

My mom was from Puerto Rico. While she didn't bring many customs with her, being a doting grandmother was one thing she wouldn't forgo.

"I will, Mommy."

"Get some rest," Mom said to me. "Or you could stop by the barbecue at the hotel. The one you said no to."

I almost growled. I'd hoped she'd forgotten.

I'd turned down the invite for the casual rehearsal dinner, saying Weezie needed sleep before the wedding. My parents knew it would be a late night and had also said no. Truthfully, tonight was for Adam's family, who had traveled here for the wedding, and we were only Rylan's adopted family.

"I don't think so." I nodded good-bye and kissed my dad on the cheek. Then I pulled my mom in for a hug to whisper, "This weekend is about Rylan. Don't do a thing to ruin it."

She pinched my arm and mouthed, *Monday.*

Monday was good. Cal would hopefully be back in New York with his date, and my mom could have a fit and yell at me then.

I didn't go to the barbecue. Instead, I went home and drank a cup of herbal tea, then took a shower before crawling into bed with a romance novel. This one was historical fiction about a duke and a seamstress. It was a stupid book about wealthy royalty falling for the help, which hit a little too close to home.

Slamming the book shut, I closed my eyes and was willing myself to fall asleep when there was a loud banging on my front door.

I didn't have to get out of bed to know who it was. I tried to ignore it, but the banging got louder, this time coupled with his shouting my name.

After tying a robe over my pajamas, I walked down the stairs and opened the door. Without waiting for a greeting or to ask if he could come in, Cal barged inside and paced my tiny hallway.

"What the fuck, Shell? You skipped the rehearsal dinner?" Then he lowered his voice. "Shit. Is Weezie here?"

I couldn't believe the liberties he was taking, yet I shook my head. "She's with my parents." Crossing my arms over my chest, I shot back, "Where's your girlfriend?"

His eyes blazed. The flecks of gold around his pupils darkened, and he looked murderous. I wasn't afraid, though.

Then Cal seemed to deflate. He leaned into the wall, running his hand through his hair. "I deserve that. Look, Shell, Sophia isn't my girlfriend. She hasn't been in a long while. She talked me into bringing her to the wedding. It was a mistake, but I couldn't send her home."

"Whatever." I started toward the kitchen. I needed a shot of bourbon, but since that wasn't a good idea for me in my condition, I'd have to settle for water.

"Shell, are you listening to me? Where the fuck were you? I sat there all night, worried something happened. I couldn't ask Rylan, and I knew Adam would slaughter me if I brought it up."

"I'm coming to the wedding tomorrow. Decided to sit tonight out."

Cal's large body loomed over me in my tiny kitchen. I didn't know whether I wanted to run to him or sprint away as fast as I could.

I guzzled the water, feeling my cheeks heat. It was the hormones. My body was reacting to the crazed side of this man, and my heart was reacting to all of him.

"What else do you want, Cal? Do you want me to thank you for saving my daughter?"

"Fuck that. No. I wanted to see you."

"You're here with another woman. I can't see you. Even if I wanted to, I couldn't see you under these circumstances."

Taking all of him in, I found myself wishing our baby had his passion and beautiful eyes. They wouldn't have his blond locks—it was unlikely with my dark curls.

"I want to be here with you." Cal stepped forward, stopping a breath away from me. "I want to be here with you all the time, but you don't call. You don't text. You never even say a quick hello. Nothing. I think about you all the time, and most of the time I wonder if you even remember me." Tiny crinkles formed around his eyes as he made his confession.

Chills ran up my spine, and my heart raced at his words.

"Are you okay?" Cal looked at me. "You're shaking."

"Cold. Hot. I don't know, but it doesn't matter. You're here with her. For the record, I think of you every moment I'm free. I think of you even when I don't want to think of you. But I can't have you."

"You can." He pulled me into his arms, his lips coming to the top of my curls. "You can. You already have me."

"Cal, don't."

"You can have me," he insisted.

"Even if I could, you don't want all of me. It's too much."

I decided it was time to drop the bomb. Cal wasn't father material, no matter what he said, let alone stepfather and father all at once.

Hugging my closer, he said, "I want every inch of you."

"I have a daughter," I said. My heart beat so fast, I was nearly dizzy. This couldn't be good for the baby.

"I fucking know. I jumped into a pool in all my clothes to grab her."

"I'm having another baby."

"The fuck?" Cal released me and stumbled backward, the vein in his temple pulsing angrily. "And you have the nerve to give me shit because I'm here with another woman? I'm back at home dreaming of when I can see you next, and you're off getting pregnant."

I almost laughed that he thought I had time to have multiple lovers. "It's yours—"

"No. No, it's not. Impossible. I haven't seen you since February. You look sexy as fuck, not pregnant. Don't you dare lie to me."

Taking a deep breath, I fought back the impulse to kick him out.

"Look, it's clear you don't know how this works. A woman learns she's pregnant around two to three weeks after it happens. Her body doesn't change much until she's three or four months along. I'm having our baby, Cal. You don't have to be a part of this, but I wanted you to know. I tried to make myself text or call, but I was afraid. I guess I was right to be nervous, since you're here with Sophia and accusing me of sleeping around."

He grabbed his forehead and hung his head. I could see his chest rising and falling with his rapid breaths. Noting he was wearing khaki pants, a charcoal-gray shirt, and Ferragamo loafers, I almost laughed at how out of place he looked here on the island. More reasons why this couldn't work.

His head shot up, and his gaze locked on mine. "I'm sorry. I didn't mean it that way. This is a shock."

"Yes, I'd hoped to tell you after the wedding . . . or I don't know when, if I'm being honest. But not like this. Not under these circumstances, with Sophia here."

"Don't mention her now," Cal said, his voice equal parts gruff and hoarse.

Changing gears, I said, "You need to go back to her right this instant." This was heading into territory I didn't want to visit.

"No. What the hell? You're not my mother. I'm staying here. We need to talk."

"Not tonight. Tomorrow is the wedding, and Rylan deserves her day. You have a guest, and I'm having a baby."

Hesitantly, he came close and pulled me into his chest. I couldn't help the long inhale I took of his expensive cologne mixed with a scent that was exclusively Cal.

"I'm not sure what to say. Most of what has come out of my mouth has been wrong, but that's my kid, so I'm sorry."

Lightly pressing my palms into his chest, I gave myself some physical space. "Yes, your kid. And mine. But now isn't the time. Go back to the hotel, please."

"How did this happen?" he said quietly.

I merely raised an eyebrow in response.

Cal huffed. "I know how it happens, but we were safe."

"Things happen," I said. I didn't add they seemed to always happen to me.

He nodded. "If you want me to leave, I will. I don't want to upset you." Then he looked at me as if I were a fragile person completely foreign to him, turned, and left.

So much for a good night's sleep like my mom suggested.

# CHAPTER ELEVEN

*Cal*

"Man on deck," I called out to announce myself as I entered the huge beachside villa the girls were getting ready in. Rylan and Shell were on the patio, so I joined them. I was trying to be as cheerful as I could. Between the bomb that Shell dropped on me last night and zero sleep, it was taking an effort.

My soon-to-be sister-in-law turned from where she was standing at the railing and rolled her eyes at that, like I knew she would. Even though I pretended to be annoyed by Rylan, I liked her. She was the type of fire my brother needed in his way-too-serious life.

I knew she was hip to something being up with Sophia and me, but she wasn't the type to intrude. Although, I suspected when the time was right, she would.

Bringing Sophia was a bad idea. I'd broken off from her, and somehow bringing her made her catch the wedding flu, as in she was going to be sick if we didn't get engaged. And I hadn't even kissed her.

"Hi, sis," I said to Rylan, determined to shut off my inner monologue.

Another eye roll came my way, but I ignored it, because standing at her side was Shell, looking like a goddess. A goddess who was carrying my baby while I worried about another woman. Shaking the nonsense from my head, I concentrated on the task at hand.

"Wanted to see if you hired a small plane and flew off the island," I told Rylan. "My brother is pacing my villa like he may never see you again."

Adam was a wreck. He wanted to marry this young, carefree woman more than anything, and was terrified something was going to prevent it.

"I'm going to check on Weez," Shell said, interrupting my conversation with Rylan. She smoothed her hand down the side of her dress and looked away from me, avoiding direct eye contact.

"See you soon," Rylan said to Shell, seemingly none the wiser.

Then, as she was leaving, Shell stopped and said softly, "Hey, Cal." When I looked up, she asked, "What's that thing called again? The hut?" She looked off toward where the wedding was taking place on the beach, pointing toward where my brother was going to get hitched in less than an hour.

"A *chuppah*," I said, using the guttural Jewish pronunciation for the *ch*. It was the traditional canopy a man and woman stood under during the wedding ceremony—and something I'd never envisioned in my future. Except, I was having a baby.

"Right." She nodded and hurried away before I could say anything else.

I guessed that was good since I wanted to hold her and kiss the fuck out of her, tell her I was going to take care of the baby and her, even though I had no freaking clue what that meant.

Pulling my attention back to her, Rylan said, "You can tell your brother that I'm right here, and more than happy to skip this whole shindig and go have a drink with him."

"Not if our mom has anything to say about it," I deadpanned.

Rylan even laughed at my joke. "I know Ruth is a bit set on the whole event. Tell your brother I'll be there, and remind him we didn't have to do this whole thing of not seeing each other before the wedding."

"Wrong," I said. "My mom is sitting in the corner of my room, alternating between giving Sophia the stink-eye and making sure Ad stays put. I'm her last chance for her son to marry a nice Jewish girl, and Sophia is neither nice nor Jewish."

I wondered what Mom would think of Shell. Not Jewish, mixed race, Catholic (I was pretty sure), fifteen years younger than me, and a single mom. She didn't tick off one box my mom had for a spouse of mine. Too bad my mom didn't value how another person made me happy, because when it came to Shell, she sure as fuck did.

Standing in front of me, wringing her hands, Rylan asked, "You sure she's not upset about that when it comes to me?"

"Nothing upsets her when it comes to Adam. He's the favorite son. If he's happy, she's happy. Plus, rumor has it you're fine with raising a Jewish family, or whatever else you promised my brother." I waggled my eyebrows at her, then lowered my gaze to her belly. "Does that mean . . ."

Wouldn't that be funny? My brother, one of the two I shared a womb with, and I were having babies at the same time.

"Would you stop staring at my wife in her robe?" came from behind me.

*Speak of the devil.*

"What are you doing here?" I asked Adam, using two fingers to point from my eyes to his, signaling I was watching him.

"Don't worry, I cleared it with Mom."

"What did I tell you?" I said to Rylan. "The favorite child."

"Go," Adam said to me. "Go back to Soph. Mom looked like she was ready to claw her eyes out."

"Shit." This couldn't be good, especially when I'd rather run to Shell than to rescue Sophia.

"Hey there, mogwai," I said to Weezie. "You behaving?"

I didn't know how to communicate with kids, but I'd give myself an A for effort. The wedding party was in full swing around the pool, and I'd found Shell and her daughter over by the cake, admiring it from afar.

Rather, Shell was trying to keep her daughter from lunging into it.

"Hi," Weezie said to me, then whispered to her mom, "Mommy, it's the man from the pool."

Shell nodded. "Yes, baby girl."

"Are you ready for cake?" I asked Weezie, but it was her mom who answered.

"We're trying to keep our distance since we haven't had dinner yet."

I shrugged. "Nothing wrong with a little cake before dinner."

Shell gave me a dirty look.

"See, Mommy?"

"Weez, this is Ry and Adam's cake. They have to cut it first and have the first bite, like on your birthday."

"Do they have to spread their pinkie across the top?"

"No, baby."

"Why not?"

I felt like a voyeur watching these two and their beautiful interaction. I knew Shell must be a good mom, but now I could see she was one of the very best when it came to patience.

"It's for good luck," Weezie said to me. "Mom has me swipe my pinkie over my name. It's a super . . . stitch . . . ion."

I nodded, vaguely remembering the tradition from when I was younger.

"Where are you sitting?" I asked Shell.

Glancing at her daughter, she said wryly, "Far away from the pool."

"Mom, you said you weren't going to tease me."

"Sorry, Weez."

"Can I go dance with *Abuelo*?"

"Typical kid, changes subjects in a quick minute," Shell said.

Sure enough, Sam was dancing by the hot tub, Marva sitting nearby.

"Yes, let me watch you walk over there."

I let out a breath when Shell said this and didn't use Weezie's dancing as an excuse to get away from me. We both watched as Weezie wound her way to Sam, and when she made it to his embrace, Shell turned to me and went right for the jugular.

"Saw your date stomp out of here."

I nodded. "She and Mom had words. Mom told her it didn't matter what she thought of her, it was clear her son didn't care for her, and that was it. Sophia said she'd stay for the ceremony and not make a scene. Of course, then she did."

Shell stood there listening, looking radiant in her sheath dress. *Fuck, is she really pregnant?*

Shaking my head, I added, "Mom wasn't wrong. I don't care for her. Sophia." My thoughts came out in fragments, my nerves getting the best of me.

"I'm sorry," Shell said, her eyes not meeting mine.

"You shouldn't be. Look at me, Shell." When she turned her face toward mine, I noted her ears were bare. "Where are your earrings?"

"I put them away. They were too much for me."

"Shell, listen. I know this isn't a good time. Ry will want to kill me when this news breaks, and her wedding reception certainly isn't the time or place, but we need to talk. How about tomorrow? I'm not running away from this."

She swallowed whatever emotion was lodged in her throat and stared at the ground. "Tomorrow is my day with Weez. Sundays, we do something special like pancakes and snuggles. Yeah, I've missed a few, but I can't tomorrow. Not with the major changes about to hit us."

"You're not coming to the brunch? First the barbecue and now this? Why are you skipping everything?"

"It's enough. I knew I couldn't do all these events with you. Be in such proximity to you. Especially after I knew you'd brought a date."

"Shell, you're coming to the brunch. Then we're going to talk. Weezie can come eat pancakes at the brunch."

We spoke in hushed voices, her breath tickling my cheek, warming me in places I didn't know I could get warm, and that said a whole fucking lot.

"We can't talk with Weezie there. She hears everything."

I couldn't help the growl escaping me. "Shell, someone will watch her. You have a bunch of friends at this hotel, like Teddi."

Shell's head whipped up so quickly, she probably gave herself whiplash. "Teddi? What does she have to do with this? And no, I can't just leave my daughter with someone."

"Teddi seems to know a lot about me and my comings and goings."

Again, Shell's gaze was downward. "We had one night of drinks, and she pulled all kinds of nonsense out of me. I'm sorry."

"Hey." I tipped her face toward mine with my index finger. "I'm not mad."

Like I carried a virus, she whipped her face away from my finger. "Not here," she said through gritted teeth.

"We're having a baby together, Shell," I said with a smile. "Pretty sure everyone is going to know about us. Now, I have to go give my best-man speech, and you need to figure out a plan for tomorrow. I have to be back in New York on Monday for work, but we'll make a plan after brunch."

I'd had enough of the back and forth with Shell. I might not know the first thing about being a dad, but I sure as hell wasn't going to be a deadbeat one.

# CHAPTER TWELVE

After a special dinner of mac and cheese and broccoli, two helpings of cake, three Shirley Temples, an hour of dancing, and a cookie or two from the dessert table, Weezie was asleep on a chair.

My dad had asked me to dance, and I agreed to one song. It was a slow song by Celine Dion, and the melancholy mood of it pooled in my belly.

My mom sat next to Weezie, rubbing her back and watching the dancers. Rylan and Adam had danced to a Justin Bieber song, and then exited the dance floor to visit with his mom. Out of the corner of my eye, I saw her gushing over Rylan, motioning to her dress and saying something to a relative. Probably how happy she was about the match. With my dad's arm around my waist, I wondered if she'd feel the same about me.

It didn't matter, though, because Cal would do right, but he wouldn't marry me.

When the song came to an end, I gave my dad a hug. "Thanks, Dad."

He kissed my cheek and said, "The honor is all mine."

I decided to say good night to Rylan and Adam before gathering Weezie. Heading toward the bar, I saw Teddi to the right of Rylan, and made a mental note to text her later. I should have figured someone would have seen Cal and me together or sniffed out a story.

"Shell!" Rylan half shouted my name as I neared. "Weezie was so perfect. Adam and I want to take her to dinner one night. Something special."

"Oh, okay. You've already spoiled her enough, though."

"Never," Rylan said.

This was the happiest I'd ever seen her, glowing as she was tucked into Adam's side. I couldn't help but glance a beat longer than necessary at him. He and Cal shared the same hair color, but that was it. Cal resembled his mom, so I assumed Adam looked like their dad, who passed away when they were little. I'd never seen a picture of their sister who was gone, but I imagined she was beautiful.

"Thank you for having us," I told Rylan. "Including us. Weezie will never forget, and my dad was so honored to walk you down the aisle."

Rylan broke free from Adam and pulled me into a bear hug. She was squeezing me so tightly, I thought she'd never let go.

"Hey, let a lady breathe," came from behind me, and I knew the voice.

"Oh my God, I'm so sorry. Emotions are getting the best of me," Rylan said, finally letting me go. To her brother-in-law, she said, "Take a chill pill, Cal. I'm hugging my friend. Go talk to Adam."

Cal scoffed. "Don't think you can boss me around, sissy."

Rylan rolled her eyes. "Ugh, this is the way he's been."

"Anyway," I said, "I'm going to take Weez home. She's asleep."

All of a sudden, I was in a hurry to get out of there. The little hairs on the back of my neck were standing up, and I knew it had to be from Teddi watching me.

"Aw, she's such a doll," Rylan said. "We'll see you in the morning?"

I guessed Rylan forgot I said I wasn't going to the brunch, and I heard Cal clear his throat.

"Of course," I said reluctantly. "Wouldn't miss it."

Although, I would rather do anything else other than see Cal—discuss our baby with Cal—but I was stuck.

"Let Adam carry Weez out for you," Rylan said, looking at her husband, whose brother was standing next to him.

But Cal interjected. "I'll do it. Don't want the groom to miss any of his wedding reception."

"Oh, Cal, are you sucking up to me?"

Rylan thought this was about her, which was good for me but bad for Cal. One thing about my girl, she hated secrets, and when this all came out—and it would—she was going to be pissed.

"Thanks, Caleb," Adam said, addressing Cal by his full name, making some point that I wasn't privy to.

"It's nothing," Cal said simply, but it was everything.

"Night, everyone," I said as cheerfully as possible before turning and giving Teddi the stink-eye. Then I headed toward my mom and Weezie, Cal in tow.

It wasn't until I was standing in front of my mom that I realized she'd know. She was like a witch that way, sniffing out the truth with the slightest of clues.

With Cal awkwardly looming next to me, I said, "Hey, Mom, I'm going to take Weez home."

My mother didn't even bother to look at me, keeping her focus on Cal.

Rather than making introductions, I cocked my thumb toward him. "Cal's going to carry her out for me."

"Isn't that nice," my mom said, an eyebrow raised. "I'm Marva," she said to Cal.

He bent and extended his hand. "Cal. Don't get up," he said, glancing at a sleeping Weezie next to my mom, her arm draped across my mom's legs.

Although the next comment was directed at me, Mom's narrowed gaze was on Cal. "I didn't know you had a friend here, Shell."

That's what she said in front of the man who up until a day or two ago was nothing more than a booty call, and now was about to be my baby daddy.

"I'm Adam's brother," Cal said, trying to redirect, but my mom was on a hunt for details, and nothing would deter her.

"Is that so?" Mom's eyes pierced Cal's with ruthless intent. "Have you known Shell long? You're the one who saved my darling granddaughter, aren't you? So, was it the right place at the wrong time, or was it the right time?"

Keeping his cool, Cal nodded. "In fact, yes. As you know, Rylan is close with your family, so by default I am. As for the saving, Weezie can swim, so it wasn't much of a saving."

Sounded like Cal was bringing out his lawyer skills, but he had no clue who he was dealing with. My mom had interrogated the best on the island and never lost.

Mom pursed her lips. "Well, thanks for helping. Shell seems to be moody lately, so beware."

My cheeks flamed. "Oh my God, Mom. Please. Here," I said to Cal while lifting Weezie and placing her in his arms.

He was clueless when it came to how to hold her, so I kept a hand under her butt so she wouldn't fall.

"She's a human, not a grocery sack," I said, biting back a smile. "Hold her tight."

He pressed my baby girl to his chest, and I let go, giving my mom a dirty look before saying, "Night."

Mom gave Cal a Cheshire-cat smile. "Nice meeting you."

"The pleasure was all mine." He had the nerve to wink at her, which made my mom blush.

"Let's go," I grumbled, trying not to stomp.

I walked around the pool, turning around every few seconds to make sure the Neanderthal still had my kid. We wound through the hotel to the open-air lobby, and despite the stiff ocean breeze, I was burning hot.

When we were finally outside, a valet took my ticket, and Cal and I stood there in silence.

"We could talk tonight," he said hopefully.

"Don't use talking and my daughter dead asleep in your arms as an excuse to get in my pants." The last part came out purposely hushed.

Thankfully, my car pulled up, and I opened the back door, taking Weezie from his arms and carefully buckling her into her booster seat.

"Tomorrow, that's what I'm offering," I said to Cal, then hurried to the driver's side.

My phone pinged as I pulled up to the Grand the next morning, Weezie chattering in the backseat about going to the pool again. Rolling my eyes at how absurd my life was, I picked up my phone and saw the text from Teddi.

Yep, I'd texted her late last night, and then told her she had to watch Weezie for me.

*I'm sorry. It slipped out because that B-I-T-C-H was there. You know I will watch Weez. Can I take her to the beach?*

Looked like my daughter's day was going to be made, while the jury was still out on mine.

I opened the car door, handed my key to the waiting valet, and went around to help Weezie.

"Mom, don't be mad. This is more fun than having pancakes at home," she said as we entered the hotel.

"I'm not mad, sweetie."

"Your face looks mad."

Kids. They didn't mince words.

"I'm not. I promise." And I wasn't. Nervous, anxious, stressed was more like it.

Seeing Weezie's face as we entered the brunch—her eyes widening at the buffet full of sweets, pancakes, fruit, and juices—settled my stomach the tiniest bit.

"You need to take some eggs too, baby girl. Brain food."

"Mom, I have eggs at home," she said as she grabbed a plate and began piling cinnamon pancakes and bacon on it.

"One or two bites," I said, and she nodded.

We sat, and the server brought coffee around. "Oh, Shell, I'm pouring the new blend. Would you like some?"

I nodded. I knew a few cups of coffee were permitted in my current state, plus I needed the soothing aroma to comfort me. Coffee always reminded me of my dad, and his calmness would be what I wanted to embody today.

"You're not eating?"

Rylan popped by the table, looking perfect in jean shorts and a pale pink tank top, a cardigan, and her sparkly new wedding band.

"I got so busy with Weezie."

I smoothed my hand over my hair. It was still straight from the day before, but I could feel the humidity wafting in from the open French doors. It wouldn't be long before it started to curl.

"Go make a plate," she said and shooed me off with her hand.

I didn't argue . . . until I arrived at the buffet and wanted to turn around. Making himself a plate was a freshly shaven Cal. Eggs and fruit covered his plate as his yummy smell wafted off him.

"Morning," he said.

I nodded and helped myself to some fruit.

"What about your pancakes?"

"Oh, Weez got hers."

"You need more than that."

"Cal, you don't know the first thing about my condition," I said, not wanting to say the word *pregnancy* aloud.

He nodded and then placed a pancake on my plate, followed by some eggs. "See you after you eat and get Weezie settled. I'm in my usual room . . . for privacy. I imagine you don't want to have this conversation around others."

I had to give it to him; the guy was slick.

It was doubtful I had anything insightful left to say, so I went to eat.

Weezie hugged Rylan good-bye and went back to gobbling up her food. I took a bite of my pancake, and it was awfully good. As if Cal had willed it, I'd just finished everything on my plate as Teddi appeared.

"Hey, Weez, want to go to the beach with me?"

"Teddi, really?" My daughter hopped out of her chair, ready to rush out the door.

I had to hand it to her, Teddi knew what she was doing too, earning brownie points with me as she swept my daughter out of here. Weezie knew Teddi because she'd hung out at my place a few times, bringing wine over for a girls' night.

Weezie bounced up and down next to me. "Oh, Mommy, can I?"

Unable to dislodge the lump in my throat, I nodded. "She just ate a huge breakfast, so I would stay out of the water for a while. Her swimsuit is on under her clothes."

"No worries. We'll pick up some seashells while we're out there."

"Oh, can you sunscreen her?"

Teddi nodded.

"See you later," the pair both hollered as they walked away.

I caught Cal out of the corner of my eye, watching the scene before slipping out too. Wiping my mouth, I set my napkin down and went to walk the plank.

I mean, talk with Cal.

# CHAPTER THIRTEEN

*Cal*

When a soft knock rapped on my door, I jumped up and pulled it open.

Under normal circumstances, I would have yanked Shell inside and kissed the fuck out of her. It wasn't like I didn't want to, but she was fragile . . . right?

Plus, things between us were uncertain.

I sure as hell felt uncertain, both inside and out. I never imagined having a child or settling down. Shell was the first woman to make me consider the possibility, but this whole insta-family part of it was daunting. I'd do the right thing, of course, but I didn't know what that was.

"Come in," I said softly.

Shell walked in and sat on the sofa. Linking her hands in her lap, she wrung her fingers as I sat across from her in the club chair.

"Look, Cal, it was never my intention to keep this from you. You have every right to know your child and be a part of their life. What I want you to know is I don't have any expectations of you."

Leaning forward, I cleared my throat. "I'm not a deadbeat."

"That's not nice." Her pupils became pinpoints as her eyes narrowed on me.

Sucking in a breath, I thought for a moment. "I'm sorry. It's not nice, but it's the truth. This baby will be provided for."

"So, you're going to throw money at me?"

The lawyer in me took pause, trying to think what she was getting at. I'd never given her the impression I was the settling-down type, so I didn't think Shell intended to rush me down the aisle.

"I just wanted to assure you that I wouldn't shirk my responsibilities."

Licking her lips, she seemed to take a deep breath. "Do you plan to be a part of the baby's life?"

A jumble of consonants and vowels clogged my throat. Did I? Unable to find the right words, I just nodded.

"You do?" she asked.

"Well, Adam lives here, so I'll see the baby when I come, if that works?"

She stood and turned toward the glass doors. If this was a test, I was failing. I thought money was what Shell wanted. Was she supposed to be tied down to a guy who lived in the States?

"Shell, look at me," I said, pushing to my feet. "I'm trying to do what you want. I don't want to upset you. I don't know a diaper from a bottle. I'm not dad material, but that doesn't mean I won't do what's right."

Whirling around, she spoke through gritted teeth. "I know you're not a deadbeat, and I don't want to force another man to commit to me because I went and got knocked up. Which was my fault. I noticed the condom broke when I slipped it off you the last time you were here, but I didn't say a word. Why? Because I know what this is. Between us, I mean."

"It did? And what is this between us?" I asked, naturally curious of her impression. She was the one who drew the boundaries, yet I was the commitment-phobic one.

"It's a booty call. Albeit a geographically undesirable one."

"Bullshit." Anger bubbled in my chest. "I think about you all the time."

She shook her head. "Don't. Let's not confuse great sex and fun times with emotions. I don't want you to abandon your bachelor lifestyle for me, but I did think you would want regular visits with your child."

There she went, drawing the line in the sand again. I'd never wanted the big house, two kids, a dog, and a wife, so I had no idea why her pushing me out of her life felt like a punch to the gut.

"You're mixing this all up, Shell. I do want to see my kid. And I want to see you. I want to do whatever you want." I took a step closer to her.

"Except commit." She looked away. "I didn't mean to say that. Like I said, I can't force you. I did that once, and look where it got me."

"Weezie—"

"Don't," Shell said. "You don't know."

I inched another step closer. We stood there, two ships about to cross paths.

"I'm not the marrying kind. Didn't see that type of shit growing up. My mother worked her ass off as a single parent, and the three of us were a handful. I cut up while Adam was the caretaker, and Becca was a loose cannon. None of it was predictable or what others had at home. So, I decided family life wasn't for me."

Shell scoffed at me. "I get the single mom part."

"Well, you won't want for anything financially."

"Just stop. This is going nowhere. I hear you, and I'll let you know how things are progressing and all that. But this is good-bye for us."

After having her say, Shell blazed past me.

Truthfully, I didn't know what she was getting so upset about. I wasn't the type of man who would swing by and grab milk on the way home from work.

"Please, Shell. I'm doing what's best."

"Okay, Cal. Okay. Well, your best isn't what I expected." She didn't stop to look at me on her way out of my room.

As the door slammed shut behind her, I knew I messed up, but it wasn't in my DNA to know how to fix it. I did what I'd tell a client to—pay up and get what they wanted.

The question was, did I want to do that?

# CHAPTER FOURTEEN

Looking toward the last table that had been sat, I froze and turned to my coworker.

"Marni, will you take that last table for me?"

She shook her head, patting her apron pocket. "Nope. He already warned me you'd ask, and tipped me to say no."

*Of course he did.*

Cal had stayed less than twenty-four hours on the island after we talked—if that's what he'd call it—and left the Monday after the wedding as planned. He'd texted that I owed him to stay in touch, and to let him know about doctor appointments.

I hadn't. It had been a week since he left, and I hadn't texted, called, emailed, or sent out smoke signals.

I was staying busy at work, helping my dad, and helping Weezie with her swimming in my free time—basically, anything but communicating with my baby daddy. My mom told me I was being stubborn, and she threatened to tell my dad.

In a last-ditch effort to get her to keep quiet for a few more weeks, I promised to message Cal. I wasn't ready yet for the disappointment I was sure I'd see on my dad's face when he learned the news.

"Welcome to Camila's. What can I get you?" I stared at the guest, hoping he'd fade away into the horizon.

"Shell, we need to talk."

Shaking my head, I said, "We definitely don't. This is between your brother and me. I can't even believe you're involved."

Adam pulled in a deep breath. "I'm involved because he's a jerk. Because he doesn't know what end is up when it comes to being there for someone. That's my role. It always has been."

Crossing my arms, a no-no when it came to serving patrons, I asked Adam, "Do you want a rum runner?" I had to move this discussion along, or else I'd sit down and tell him exactly what I thought of his brother.

"No, I don't want a rum runner. I want you to call Cal. He's an ass who messed up. I know this because every work call we have turns into a Shell-centered discussion. Rylan is getting impatient with me over my long calls because we're leaving for London next week on our honeymoon. And I don't like keeping secrets from her."

"Yeah, what happened? I thought you were leaving a few days after the wedding?" Just like me, Rylan had secrets I wanted to know.

"We pushed it back. I had to take care of a few things."

I glared at him.

"Shell, I'm not the one you should be mad at. I'm advocating for you. After our honeymoon in London, Ry and I are back in Michigan for the summer, so I won't be here to keep an eye on you. You need Cal. Don't get me wrong, I told him to man up. It's obvious he cares for you, because he's never worried about anyone a day in his life. He's usually the fucker who fucks shit up, pardon my French."

I scoffed. "Well, he fucked this up. He thinks all I want is a sugar daddy. I'm not looking to tie him down, but he could want to know his kid. To be in his or her life."

Running his hand through his hair, Adam blew out a long breath. "He was wrong. The fact is, he's scared. My brother doesn't even have a goldfish. He's New York's best divorce attorney and thinks everything starts and ends with money. Call him. He's too chickenshit to reach out, but he's a mess."

Swallowing the emotions I didn't want to have—like feeling sorry for a scared Cal—I said, "I don't believe your brother is chickenshit about anything."

"Shell, he's never bought anyone jewelry before. Clothes, fancy purses, extravagant weekends, yes, but never a jewel. Always thought it was too personal."

The guilt made me look away.

Switching gears, Adam asked, "How are you feeling?"

"I heard the heartbeat," I blurted excitedly in a moment of weakness.

Adam both smiled and shook his head. "Call my brother. You can't do this to him."

"Me?"

He stood, tossing a tip on the table.

"Anything else?" I asked, delivering it with a bit of snark.

"Take the job with your dad. My brother may be an asshole, but there's no way he's going to put up with you working on your feet all day while carrying his baby."

I snatched up the tip, rolling my eyes at his back, then hurried to check on a table I'd ignored.

Later that night, after I'd tucked Weezie in and made myself a cup of herbal tea, I picked up my phone. In my mind, I started to craft a text, but there was no way to shorten all I had to say. Before I could chicken out, I forced myself to dial his number.

"Shell, are you okay?" Cal answered without saying hello, his sexy voice rumbling over the line.

"I'm fine." For a second, I felt bad for him, and then I remembered our last "discussion."

A long stretch of silence passed between us.

"Is this a bad time?" I finally asked.

"No. I'm at the office, just looking over some paperwork for tomorrow."

"I didn't mean to interrupt you."

"Shell, don't. It's fine. I'm glad you called. I've wanted to call every day to apologize for how I acted, but I wasn't sure you could forgive me."

"Your brother came to see me," I said, moving the conversation along.

"Shit," Cal muttered.

"He's anxious for us to set the news free. I'm going to show soon. I heard the heartbeat, so it's time."

"What?" Cal's voice boomed over the line.

"I heard the heartbeat. It was very fast and strong."

"I'm coming to see you. I want to hear it."

"What?" I asked, not sure I'd heard correctly. "Cal, we need to figure out a plan, not make travel arrangements."

Another long pause stretched out over the line.

"I'm texting my assistant now," he said, "and having him book me a flight for tomorrow. I'm coming to see you and hear our baby. Then I want to have a different discussion with you, one where I make you happy."

"You can't just come here."

"Yes, I can. Also, pack a bag or something. You'll spend a few days with me at the Grand."

"But Weezie . . ."

"She'll come too. I'll get a suite for us. She'll love it."

Reeling, I thought, *Wow, this came out of nowhere.*

"We're not staying in a hotel with you, Cal. That's not appropriate."

"See you tomorrow. Can you book the doctor for us?"

A frustrated growl came from me and through the phone.

"Shell? Are you okay?"

"No. No, I'm not."

"Well, call your mom? Do you need to see a doctor?"

"Cal," I said before blowing out a long breath. "Stop this. I'm having whiplash from you. You want to send me money, then your brother says you're too scared to call, so I call. Then you're booking vacations with me and my daughter. I can't do things like this. I have to work this week. Weezie has school. You have to work. In New York."

My words came out in choppy sentences, my lungs having trouble getting the air out and back in.

"You should quit your job," he said matter-of-factly. "How will you take care of the baby?"

Another growl came from me.

"I take it you don't like that idea," he said.

"What makes you think that?" I spat out.

At this point, I was pacing my bedroom.

"Caleb," I said, trying to calm down and get him to focus. "Listen. We're having a baby. If you want to be a part of the baby's life, I won't stop you, but—"

Interrupting me before I could add that he couldn't take over my life, he said, "Good. I'll see you tomorrow, and we can go to the doctor."

I tried to assert myself again, but Cal insisted he had to go because he was booking the flight his assistant sent over.

Falling back on my bed, I closed my eyes and wished that had gone differently. Ricky might be a deadbeat, but Cal was bossy, confusing, and infuriating.

# CHAPTER FIFTEEN

I spent the next morning delivering beans for my dad. After that, I went to the Grand first in an effort to avoid the dad-to-be, who was soon to be checking in, and then ran by the Ritz and stopped at a few restaurants.

I always spent a few minutes talking to the manager, asking how they liked certain blends, what other types of beverage products they were using, and if they had any constructive feedback. I'd been hearing a lot about flavored beans, and I knew my dad wasn't going to go for it, so I'd started researching syrups.

I hadn't brought up the idea to my dad because I wanted to have a plan before I decided to quit waitressing.

A small spark had formed inside me for a branded line of syrups called Island Girl Flavors. It was a pipe dream, but I had to think of a life where I didn't wait tables and could afford to keep my children fed. The syrups could be added to coffees, creamers, or espresso drinks. I had some experience with making simple sugar, and I was studying how to add flavor correctly. I also knew I could ask Rylan or Teddi to help me with some mixology.

The problem was capital. I didn't have any.

I was so deep in thought about a special coconut syrup that I didn't notice who was standing in Island Coffee when I blew through the door.

"Hi, baby," my dad said, forcing me to look up. "Adam's brother is here." My dad smiled, like he'd suddenly fallen in love with Cal.

"I–I see that."

"He wants to get in on the expansion with Adam. Thinks we can export to the States and other islands. Mom-and-pop businesses are popular."

I cocked an eyebrow at Cal. "Is that so?"

He smirked. "Sure is. I could get it a placement on *Real Housewives*."

Waving my hand in the air, I said, "I've had enough of this silliness. Seriously. Enough."

Heading straight to the back, I went to the fridge and took out a Coke. Holding the glass bottle to my forehead, I breathed in and out, counting to five with every inhale and exhale. Dad followed me, frowning.

"Don't be rude," my dad said low. "They're trying to help. The Stern brothers are the answer to having something of your own."

If he only knew.

I didn't have a chance to answer because Cal also appeared in the back too, saying he was going to head out.

"Do you have a car here?" he asked me, and I nodded. "Any chance you could give me a ride to the Grand? Jack had to do an airport run."

Frowning, I said, "You could have rented a car," but when my dad pointedly cleared his throat at my rudeness, I quickly changed my tune. "No problem. Let's go."

Between being scolded by my father and Cal bossing me around, I felt like my cheeks were on fire. After downing my Coke, I tossed the bottle in a recycling bin before walking toward the door. Once we were outside, I wished my hair wasn't in a bun but down to shield my face and hide my emotions.

"Where are you parked?" Cal asked like we were a couple out on a jaunt.

"Around the corner. Come on. I have to get Weez from school, and then I work at Camila's tonight. My mom is watching her."

"Shell, quit that shitty job. I'll pay the difference."

I shook my head just as we arrived at my little car. "I know it's not a fancy Jeep like you're used to. Hope this will do," I said snidely, finding myself in a fighting mood.

Ignoring me, Cal walked toward the driver's door. "I'll drive."

"What?"

"I said I'll drive. Have to keep up with my skills. I'm going to be here often."

"Hope you survive being behind the wheel of a jalopy," I muttered as I slapped the keys in his waiting hand.

"Hush, Shell," he said, folding himself in the driver's side.

I slid into the passenger seat and refused to look at him. Cal's profile was handsome enough, and being near him did things to my libido. I told myself it was the pregnancy hormones.

As Cal steered us toward the Grand, he then dove right in. "Did you call the doc?"

"It doesn't work that way. I have another appointment in a few weeks. I can't just call and demand to be seen. It costs money."

"Good, then I'll pay like Adam did."

"What?" I whipped my head toward him.

"Shit," Cal mumbled, not meeting my eyes for a second. Sighing, he gave in and spilled it. "Okay, so Rylan's pregnant. It's very early, so Adam paid to hear the heartbeat, and then he refused to leave for London until they heard it again. They haven't told anyone."

Both thrilled for them and furious at Rylan for keeping the secret from me, I blew out a breath. "That's why he was so cagey . . . the little shits."

"I don't know what you're going on about, but I guess it doesn't matter. I want to hear our baby, and then I want to take you to dinner in front of everyone and let it be known you're with me."

My eyes wide and my breath caught in my throat, I had to remind myself not to fall for his spiel. They were just words.

"Are you with me?" I asked quietly.

Cal gave me a serious glance. "I'm here."

The next morning, Cal picked me up himself in a Jeep. Adam's, he said as he walked me to the passenger side. The night before, he'd sat at Camila's all night keeping an eye on me as I worked, ordering food and asking that I join him.

The whole thing was absurd. He'd gone way over the top in an effort to self-correct. I didn't have to be a genius to understand.

"Do you know the address? I can put it in the GPS," Cal said, interrupting my walk down last night's memory lane.

"I'll just direct you."

This way, our ride was filled with a lot of *make a right, go around the roundabout, take the second exit,* and *right up there* instead of false promises. I knew Cal was going to make some kind of declaration, and all of a sudden, I didn't want that.

Parked in the small lot next to the hospital building, Cal turned. "I'm trying, Shell. This is new to me. A shock."

I nodded and got out of the car.

He rounded the front to catch up with me, and we went inside. The nurse hadn't understood when I called and asked for an ultrasound because I'd just been in for one. She kept asking if there was a problem. When I'd said we would self-pay for another, she'd immediately booked it and said to bring a check or credit card.

"Welcome back, Mrs. Light. Glad we could accommodate you," the nurse said when registering me.

While we waited, I explained to Cal. "I'm about nine or ten weeks along. In a few weeks, they'll be able to hear the heartbeat through the belly, but last week when I was here, they used a vaginal wand. I don't want you to be alarmed."

He looked pale but nodded.

"You can look away and just listen."

This time he shook his head.

"Mrs. Light?" a technician called out in the waiting room.

"Are you going to get rid of his last name?" Cal whispered as we walked through the door.

"I don't know. It's Weezie's name too."

He nodded then and looked straight ahead.

In the exam room, seated next to my head, Cal looked like he might faint. A green hue had colored his skin. His fist was clenched at his side, and I made a note to have the birth without him present.

"There it is. There's your baby's heartbeat. Listen to it, strong and fast," the tech said with a smile.

I watched Cal's profile and saw what I thought was a smile, his eye crinkling in the corner.

"Is that normal?" he asked. "It's so fast."

"It is, Mr. Light."

"That's not my name." Cal obviously tried to soften his clipped tone, but it didn't help.

The technician looked up, frowning. "Oh, I'm sorry. I assumed . . ."

"Stern. Caleb Stern. Thank you for explaining. Can we hear a bit longer?"

She nodded. After a minute or so, I was starting to feel uncomfortable lying there with a vaginal wand stuck up my hoo-ha.

"I'm finished," I finally said.

The technician removed the wand and then slipped out of the room without saying anything, probably because of Cal's dressing-down.

"Would you mind stepping out so I can clean up and get dressed?" I asked him.

Cal nodded, unusually quiet. "I'll be in the waiting room."

I took my time, and it wasn't until I'd made it back to the waiting room to join Cal that I realized he'd made a huge effort. This wasn't something he had to do, not something he'd ever imagined doing, and yet he'd done it.

"Thank you," he said to me. "Our baby sounds like he's a fighter."

"He?"

"That's what I think."

I smiled and let it go.

Outside, Cal pulled me into his side, walking his arm around me. "You ever been to New York?"

"No. I've only been to Miami and Orlando."

"You should come visit. If you can," he said as we approached the passenger door. "But first, dinner tonight."

"You don't have to," I told him as he slid in.

"Eye of the Sea, seven o'clock. Adam said he's telling Rylan later today. Sorry, but he can't wait, and promised they would watch Weezie if you needed."

He sped out of the lot, the top down. Wind whipped around us, and shorter strands of my hair came loose from my bun.

"Whoa, Cal, you can't arrange for childcare."

"Shell, Adam's going to be your family," he said, and I gasped.

Glancing at the look on my face, he laughed out loud. "I'm not proposing."

I felt like a fool. Of course he wasn't proposing.

"What I meant was you're giving birth to his nephew."

"Or niece," I shouted over the wind.

"Or niece. So, Adam is family. He and Rylan can watch Weezie."

"My mom has her bridge game, so that would actually be good," I said, correcting my blunder.

I had to get along with Cal, I reminded myself. With Ricky was out of the picture, I needed support. However much Cal wanted to give.

"Good, I'll send Jack for you, and Adam can pick up Weez. This keeps things between us quiet from the little one until you break the news. Soon."

The sky was Caribbean blue, the air salty, as we drove along Seven Mile Beach. I never thought I'd be so stressed in the most beautiful place on the planet.

"Bossy, much?" I asked, and Cal snorted.

"Get used to it."

I clicked on the radio in an effort to ignore his charming orders. No one had ever cared for me a day in my life when I was married to Ricky. While I knew this wasn't marriage or close to it, it was the best I was going to have in my current situation.

# CHAPTER SIXTEEN

*Cal*

"Hey, Jack," I said into the speakerphone as I toweled off from my shower. I'd gone for a long run when I got back from the doctor's appointment.

As if hearing a beating heart growing inside another person wasn't shocking enough, contemplating a marriage proposal was enough to take me down. When I'd said Adam was family, I meant by default.

But then the idea of spending a lifetime with Shell hit me.

Shell—a woman who didn't care about my money or accolades or prestige or what I could give her financially. Shell—a woman who cared about devotion, which was something I wasn't sure I had inside me to give anyone.

"You there, Cal?"

"Yeah, sorry . . . got distracted. I need you to go over to Shell's and bring her back here by seven. Taking her to dinner."

"You coming with?"

Tying the towel around my waist, I said, "No. I'll meet her in the lobby."

Jack huffed. "This a date or what?"

"What are you, my mom?" I asked, annoyed. I was paying him to drive, not give his advice.

I looked in the mirror as I spoke and saw a dozen new wrinkles in my forehead, thanks to hearing the baby's heartbeat. Yeah, men look in the mirror, especially when they're about to become a father at forty-one with no clue how to handle the responsibility of a dog, let alone a baby.

Jack chuckled. "Nah, just saying if it's a date, don't you think you should come with?"

"I'll meet her here, but thanks."

I needed time to collect myself, drive off any thoughts of proposing or whatever spell Shell was putting on me. I was going to take her to dinner, treat her right, and make sure everyone knew she was with me . . . that she was carrying my baby. Even if I didn't want to commit full-time, no one else was swooping in on my territory.

Shaking my head at my own awful thoughts, I decided I was who I was.

"Okey-dokey," Jack said, trying not to laugh.

"See you later." I disconnected the call and thought about what I meant to achieve by taking Shell out.

I was claiming her. Except, I didn't think this was the right way, but I didn't know how else to accomplish it.

"Wait!" I called out to Jack as he was walking toward the Jeep. "I'm coming with you."

He only nodded. "Saw you driving your brother's ride earlier. Thought I was out of a job," he joked as he slid in the car.

"Borrowed it, but Rylan took it back to him."

"Glad you decided to pick your date up. That was gonna be an awkward ride for me."

I let out a nervous chuckle. "Well, I wouldn't want that." I also didn't want anyone else to make a play for my girl.

When we sped off, I was grateful for the windows being open, so it was too loud to talk.

At Shell's, I held up a *wait right here* finger for Jack as I made my way to the door.

I didn't have to knock because Shell was sitting on the porch, wearing a yellow off-the-shoulder sundress, her hair in long dark waves down her back, and her legs stretched out in front of her, a sad look on her face.

Before I could ask what was wrong, she said, "Weez left about ten minutes ago. She just went off like it was nothing. Holding Adam's hand and walking toward his car without looking back, a skip in her step. She's not even concerned over leaving me."

Shell looked off toward the distance, and I thought for a moment she was going to cry. Then she waved a hand in front of her face and explained. "It's the hormones. They're getting the best of me."

She stood quickly, and I caught a glimpse of the earrings I'd bought her. I smiled, wondering where the anklet was.

I chuckled. "I'm pretty sure Weezie is swayed by bottomless Shirley Temples and chicken fingers when it comes to Adam and Rylan. I don't think you need to worry," I said, taking her hand in mine.

Coming along to pick her up had been the right thing to do. Although, I wouldn't tell Jack that.

"You look beautiful," I told her, my lips grazing her cheek and moving on to her mouth.

We pressed our lips together a few times until she pulled back.

"Cal, I don't know. It's all so confusing to me."

The old me wanted to reply, *It was never confusing before*, but I held back.

Instead, I said, "I understand, but know this—the attraction is there. The chemistry is off the charts. That hasn't changed."

Shell gave me a frustrated look. "I'm changing. You know, my body? I'm going to get big, and then it takes a while to get back to where I was, and well, by then it may not matter." She turned her face from me.

"With my baby. You're getting big with my baby," I said out of nowhere.

It finally dawned on me how sexy she would be with my little one growing in her. It also occurred to me that I had no clue who I was anymore.

"Big with my baby," I said again, awestruck at the thought. "That's sexy as fuck."

Shell glanced at me. "Last time, it was easier. I didn't know what to expect. But now I do."

"Well, I don't, so it's all new to me. Come on, let's get you to dinner where you can relax." I had no clue where any of this solicitude was coming from, but it seemed right.

I took her hand and walked with her toward the car.

Jack hopped out to open the front door for her as he greeted her. "Why don't you ride in front, so your hair doesn't blow as much."

I felt myself growl. *Why is he suggesting that? Shouldn't that be me?*

The ride back to the hotel was quiet other than the wind reverberating throughout the Jeep. Along the way, my thoughts warred with my heart and other parts of my body. I wanted to hurry up and eat, and then carry Shell back to my room like a caveman, but that wasn't possible.

Seated at Eye of the Sea, we were at a primo table in the back, the ocean roaring through the open glass panels. Our table was covered in a pristine white tablecloth, and servers attended to our every need. It was the type of place people went when they wanted to impress, except Shell wasn't the type impressed by that kind of thing.

"Sparkling water?" I asked Shell as the server approached, and she nodded.

I ordered a bottle of sparkling water for her and a Scotch for myself. The server asked if Shell wanted lemon or lime, and she requested both. I banked that tidbit in my memory vault, sensing that knowing little things like that about her was important.

Like how someone took their coffee.

"Weezie? She's five?" I asked.

"Almost six, going on thirty-five," Shell said. "She's had to grow up way too much in the last few months. I just want her to be a kid, but now she wants to know things she should never have to know about."

Understanding, I nodded. "Like when our dad died, I think my mom felt the same. We were too young to deal with that. Just babies."

"Yeah," Shell said wistfully. "I wish it was different for Weez, but we're dealing. This baby will be another blow."

From somewhere I couldn't explain, I said, "We'll make it okay for her." I didn't have the first clue how, or if it was even my place, but it came out of my mouth.

"Oh," Shell said. "I will. She'll enjoy the chance to be a bossy big sister, but I know she'll miss some of the attention."

"That's the thing with being a triplet, you're used to sharing attention," I told her. "It's weird. I've never thought much about it, but sitting here with you, I'm thinking about it. It was the only way I knew. We had our roles, you know . . . I was the fun one."

"Of course you were." Her laughter rang through the restaurant, and I wanted to keep it all for myself.

We were interrupted when the server returned with the water and my Scotch.

In an effort to get rid of any intruders, I asked Shell, "How's the tasting menu sound?"

She nodded, then told the server, "No soft cheese for me."

He nodded and scooted away, sensing my command of the situation.

Once Shell had squeezed some lime and lemon into her water, I said, "Cheers."

When she returned the sentiment, my heart pounded like we were celebrating more than just this moment.

# CHAPTER
# SEVENTEEN

*Shell*

"Thank you," I said to Cal, and I meant it. "I've never eaten here, and it was worthy of all the hype. Plus, that was really civilized," I added, staring over my cup of herbal tea.

The ocean lapped in the distance, and the stars twinkled happily outside the open window next to our table. It was like a scene out of a movie—not my life.

Of course, Cal being Cal, he leaned back in his chair and winked, looking like the cat who ate the canary.

A past version of me would have retracted my statement, but he was trying. He'd brought me to the nicest place on the island—Eye of the Sea—and waited patiently while I enjoyed every course. I was sure he did this sort of thing all the time in Manhattan, but this was a first for me.

"That's what I wanted," he said, leaning forward with his elbows resting on the table. "Actually, what I want isn't civilized at all."

The last part came out more like a whisper, meant only for me, and I shivered.

"Shell." My name was practically a growl in his throat, and my body pulsed with want.

Desire raged in my belly, and I told myself it was pregnancy hormones as I clenched my thighs, trying to tamp the coursing fire. Like a fool, I took a sip of my hot tea, thinking it would douse the heat burning inside me, but no such luck.

"Shell, I don't know what to do. I'm going about this all wrong. I know that, but I also know I want you. So fucking bad. Nothing feels like when I'm with you. I'd sit in New York after seeing you, trying to recreate the feeling I felt when I was with you, and I couldn't."

I shook my head and was about to interrupt when he spoke again.

"No, don't say anything. Don't argue with me. I know I'm making unrealistic requests and demands—all of it too little, too late—but that's me. I don't know what I'm doing when it comes to building a relationship. I only understand taking them apart."

Every cell in my body wanted to believe the forlorn divorce lawyer in front of me, but what was he asking?

When I breathed out his name, Cal stood.

"Let me call Adam and ask if they want to keep Weezie for the night, please?" he whispered while bending down toward me. "I need to feel you, touch you, be with you. Please."

I had no idea when he came up with this idea.

"You can't make those kinds of requests. Weezie is mine—she's only stayed with my mom and dad. She doesn't know Adam and Rylan like that."

I'd long ago set my tea down, and now I stood from my chair, facing Cal. He tipped my chin up with his index finger.

"I know. It's wrong of me, but I can't help it. I'm going back to New York tomorrow afternoon, and I need you." His fingers intertwined with mine.

"Another reason why we can't—you're leaving. I'm already having your baby. A piece of you is permanently intertwined in my life. Forever. I have to keep my own feelings out of it."

We stood there next to our table in the back of the restaurant, overlooking the ocean, several hundred dollars charged to Caleb's room, discussing our next move. It felt like a farce—I'd already slept with the man. Many times. I was knocked up with his kid, and now I wanted to play hard to get. Why?

"There's no happily-ever-after for us," I blurted.

He pulled me into him, my eyelashes brushing his white shirt. "There may be. I don't know. I can come visit a lot, right?"

I didn't respond. It felt like an impossible fairy tale.

"Let's go to my villa for a while," he said softly. "I can have a drink and you can have some sparkling water, and then Jack will take you home. You can pick Weezie up on your way home."

Cal sounded defeated, and like the fool I was, I felt bad for him.

I took my phone out of my purse and noted the time—nine thirty—and the text from Rylan saying Weezie was asleep on her couch and Adam was carrying her to a guest room.

Cal's intentions suddenly felt premeditated, but I didn't care. Of course, Rylan also mentioned needing to call me tomorrow to *get all caught up*. A not-so-subtle request for all the details about my baby daddy and me.

"Actually, Weezie is asleep at Rylan's," I said without thinking. Apparently, my mouth had a mind of its own and was subtly suggesting I spend the night with him.

Another yank pulled me into his embrace, and then Cal walked me out of the restaurant with his arm around me toward the open-air lobby. I knew his villa was on the other side, and I wished he'd taken the route by the pool.

Teddi eyed me from the lobby bar, stars in her eyes. As Cal paraded me through the hotel, I knew the staff all thought *there goes another one*.

Like Rylan, I was getting lucky with a rich American, but Rylan had been a rich American at one point herself. Me, I was an island girl of mixed heritage and had two baby daddies.

This wasn't a Disney story. It was more *have a good time and see you around*, but what did I have to lose? Everyone would know we'd had an affair. The proof would be here in a few months, so why shouldn't I enjoy myself?

As we made our way to Cal's room, his palm caressed my bare shoulder, gently guiding me while I texted Rylan. She was going to keep Weezie overnight and bring her to me for breakfast. It all felt too easy, too planned, but my heart was for it, so my brain didn't care.

He unlocked and held the door for me when we arrived, and I walked into the palatial villa, curtains billowing in the breeze. The bedroom had been turned down . . . a flower surrounded by chocolates lay on the bed. The lights were dimmed, and the music set to R&B. I seemed to remember guests could request what type of music they wanted, and for the second time, I suspected this was all orchestrated by the man in front of me.

"It's so pretty here," I said while turning in a circle, taking it all in. "I imagine that's why people fall in love with coming here."

"Not me. I like coming here for you." Cal was behind me, his breath hot on my neck. "Shell, turn around."

Sade crooned in the background, and as usual, I listened to Cal. As soon as I swiveled to face him, his mouth was on me, his arm around my back, holding me steady. I could tell he was being gentle.

"You're not going to hurt me. Or the baby," I whispered.

This prompted him to slide his palm up my back and yank my head back by my hair. It didn't hurt, especially as his mouth came down on my neck and licked its way to my clavicle and back up. His head dropped lower and he pulled my dress aside, revealing my already swollen breast. His lips attached to my nipple and sucked.

I yelped. That *did* hurt.

Immediately, he pulled back. "Shit, Shell. I didn't mean . . . I don't know. This is new."

His smirk disappeared as he dropped his hands to his sides. When he backed away, I padded closer. Once I'd closed the distance between us, I boldly took his hand and used it to cup my breast, and he held me gingerly.

"They're tender. Prepping to be used for purposes other than pleasure," I told him. "That doesn't mean you can't touch me, but maybe just a tad more gently. I'm extra sensitive."

He nodded, lowering his head, this time cupping my breast over my dress and running his tongue around the exposed part of my skin. A moan escaped me, and he kept at it.

Cal slid back up my body to meet my mouth. "Was that okay?" he asked as his palm grazed my stomach, and I nodded. He kissed me, breaking away to moan, "My baby. I can't . . . it's a lot."

I couldn't respond because he went back to my lips, parting them with his tongue. Our mouths connected with a fervor while his hand continued to stay on my belly.

"I want you," he murmured. "So bad."

"Have me," I said, and he guided me toward the bed.

With reverence, he helped me sit down before kneeling in front of me and swooping my dress over my head. I didn't feel exposed like I thought I should. Rather, I watched as Cal continued to lean before me, bringing his mouth to my belly this time. He placed a kiss over my navel, lingering for a beat, and then another kiss and another pause.

I let him have his time. Then he gently pushed me back onto the bed, while not getting up himself.

His hands slid under the strings on the sides of my panties and yanked them down like a starved man. Then his mouth was on my center, tasting and nipping, neither too soft nor too gentle.

When his mouth met my core, I almost went off right then and there. A few more strokes of his tongue was all it took, and I was seeing stars.

I squirmed, needing to break free because the release was so overwhelming, but Cal kept me in place, softly taking it all from me. My eyelids fell closed, and I was floating off somewhere until I felt him creep up the bed next to me, then kiss me, tasting of me.

"Pregnancy makes it all a bit more spectacular," I mumbled.

"I see that, and here I was thinking I was that good." He laughed while speaking into my mouth, and the rumbles hit every inch of me down to my toes.

My hands slid down his back and up beneath his shirt, feeling his smooth skin and chiseled muscles. Like a well-practiced machine, he leaned back so I could unbutton his dress shirt. As he shrugged it off, my lips connected with his chest, my tongue drawing small circles around his nipple, and his head fell back.

I traced my way down his abdomen, scooting by his side in nothing but my strapless bra. Making quick work of unbuckling his belt and pants, I yanked them down. Next came his boxer briefs before I took all of him in my grasp, being as rough as I remembered he liked it.

I didn't have much time to return favors because before I knew it, I was being lifted up and laid on the pillows. Cal propped over me, his hand bracing him on the bed, his arm straight and strong, holding him up.

"Protection?" I managed to choke out.

"For what?" he asked, his brow furrowed.

"Disease?"

He came down to his forearm, his hand sweeping my hair off my face, and laughed. "Darling Shell, there hasn't been anyone since the holidays for me. You ruined me for anyone else."

I swallowed my disbelief and nodded. There were no words to explain how I was feeling because my emotions were too much. Too grand.

Cal took my nod as the permission it was and slid inside me, stopping to savor the feeling, I assumed. After all, it was what I was doing.

"Shell, fuck," he said, my name and the curse a melody on his lips.

He started to move . . . long, deep, and slow, then faster.

"You feel like heaven," he muttered, and I believed him.

"Caleb," I said, calling him by his full name like I'd done on nights before. Evenings in the past when I'd thought this was for fun.

As he drove into me now, though, I scolded myself for thinking right now was anything more than fun. Cal was caught up in the moment, as was I.

He whispered more sweet nothings in my ear, talking of visits and bedroom rounds to come. I absorbed it all as he drove into me, until I couldn't take the sensations anymore and came apart.

Not far behind me, Cal poured into me, riding it out until falling to my side. "God, you're going to kill me, Shell. I'm an old man."

I laughed. "You're not old. Forty-one isn't—"

"Too old to just become a father," he said, his words like an ice bucket dumped over my head on a hot day.

Stiffening, I sniffed back a tear and sat up. "I'm going to clean up. Can you ask Jack to take me home, so I can get some rest before getting Weezie?"

"Shell, don't. I told you I don't know what I'm doing."

Shaking my head, I murmured, "Save it," and went straight to the bathroom to get a washcloth.

As soon as I was cleaned up, I came back out and snatched up my dress. "Fun time's over. Time for me to go back to being a mom."

With his hands held up in surrender, Cal nodded. At least he knew better than to argue with a pregnant woman in the middle of the night. He called Jack and walked me to the lobby.

There, I kissed him on the cheek and said, "Thanks."

"I'm going to come with you—"

"No. I'm tired. Good night, Cal. Safe travels tomorrow."

I turned and walked out to the Jeep, grateful the lobby bar was closed and Teddi wasn't there to witness my freak-out.

Every cell in my body wanted to turn around and see Cal one more time, but this time, my brain won out, forbidding it.

# CHAPTER EIGHTEEN

*Cal*

Slowing my treadmill to a walk, I cursed through clenched teeth. Not even a punishing five miles could stop the freight train of thoughts barreling through my brain.

I'd returned home from the Caymans nearly four weeks ago, and I'd wanted to go back every day. My ego wouldn't allow it, though, not after Shell left my villa in such a hurry. She couldn't wait to get away from me that night. The saying *turnaround is fair play* hit home. How many times had I left a woman in their bed wishing for more?

Of course Shell couldn't wait to get away from me. I was an asshole. I came inside her and then admitted out loud that I was too old to be a father. *While she was carrying my child.*

I reminded myself of the details daily, and then I made myself feel better by trying to rationalize my behavior. I was scared shitless. Didn't she know that?

Bringing the treadmill to a stop, I took a swig of water and walked toward the en-suite bathroom in my office. I'd put in the treadmill a few years ago. It saved on time traveling to and from the gym, and allowed me to get a run in whenever I could. Lately, it had been often. Midday, after work, later in the evening, I was constantly battling the worry and self-doubt in my head. Between the sexual frustration and impatience when it came to not hearing from Shell, I was practically a hormonal teenager.

I turned on the water and let the steam billow into the bathroom before stepping into the shower and going over this week's schedule in my head. Adam had been in last week on his way home from his honeymoon.

"We're going to have babies around the same time. Rylan's over the moon," the fucker had the nerve to say.

Of course she was. He'd spilled the good news, and I was sure Shell had told Rylan the bad news: she was pregnant, and I wasn't going to be involved.

I wanted to punch Adam in the face at his happiness, not to mention his cavalier attitude. He was married and had wanted a family, and now he was getting it. I was supposed to be the good-time guy, and had never, ever imagined this scenario for myself.

Although, nothing was a good time these days. I didn't fuck. I didn't go to see Shell. I didn't know how Shell's three-month appointment went.

Just the week before, she'd texted me she was feeling fine and had an upcoming appointment. I texted back for her to keep me posted—like an ass, that's all I wrote.

I didn't tell her I missed her, or that I thought of her and the baby all the time. I didn't text for her to say hi to Weezie—who, by the way, was apparently excited to be a big sister. Another tidbit I'd learned from Adam, who heard while on his honeymoon. Apparently, he spoke to Shell more from London than I had. Lately, all I did was work, drink, and run.

Turning the water off, using a little bit too much force, I dried off and put my suit back on, then tossed my sweaty workout clothes in a hamper. My laundry service would pick it up for me.

*What a spoiled prick I am. Shell probably does all her own laundry.*

This was what happened at every turn, every twist of my thoughts. I thought about what Shell did.

I told myself it was a reminder of how different our lives were and how we wouldn't work, but my heart thought differently. It wanted to be with Shell, to provide for her and Weezie and our unborn son. Yes, I was convinced it was a boy.

Back at my desk, I cracked open a protein drink from the mini-fridge and looked at my emails. Another celebrity divorce case had found its way to me, representing the wife this time, and there was a communication from the husband's studio, requesting a statement.

"Go fuck yourself," I muttered to the laptop. I didn't make statements about my clients to studios.

I was getting ready to reply when my personal phone rang.

Seeing the caller ID, I muttered to myself, "About fucking time," then answered with, "Shell, you okay?"

"Yeah. Hi, Cal, how are you?"

"I'm fine. Tell me about you." I didn't say I was losing my shit over her and wanted to run to her, but she hadn't asked me to come.

"I had my doctor's appointment." Her voice was like a salve to my aching heart, a Ricola cough drop soothing a sore throat.

"And?"

"Everything looked good. I'm just thirteen weeks and out of the riskiest time. Heartbeat was still fast and strong. They can hear it through my abdomen now. Doctor wants me to make sure to eat all my meals because I didn't gain any weight this month. But mostly, they want me to keep up my strength."

"You need to quit your job. I'll take care of you so you can be good to yourself."

"Cal," she said, my name coming out like a growl. "That's not your choice. I'll take care of myself and be good for the baby, okay? But no, I'm not quitting. Is that all you have to say? No other questions?"

Leaning back in my chair, I closed my eyes. "No, that's not it. I'm torturing myself here, Shell. I can't sleep or think straight. I want to see you. To feel our baby growing inside you. But you basically kicked me out."

Silence hung heavy on the other side of the call.

"Shell?"

"I'm here. I kicked *you* out? You said you were too old to be a dad."

"I am, but that doesn't mean I'm not going to be one. That I don't want to be one, I mean."

"Your moods are too volatile, Cal. You can't be aloof one minute and downright territorial the next. Which is it? I already have a missing baby daddy from my first kid. Doing this without you doesn't scare me."

"Okay, I'll be territorial all the time. I'm coming to see you."

She blew out a long breath. "I can't have every call to you end in a surprise visit. That can't be your answer to everything."

"This isn't a surprise. I'm telling you I'm coming. I want to see you and Weezie, and take everyone out and celebrate. Don't argue. This is what I'm doing."

After another few beats of silence, she said, "Don't boss me."

"I'm not. I'm telling you. Again. I'm coming to see you. As soon as we hang up, I'm getting a flight."

"Caleb, you're confusing me."

"When I get there, it won't be confusing."

I had no idea how I was going to make that happen, but I would.

The next morning, I landed on Grand Cayman, rumpled from having to sit in coach, and tired as shit from a bad night's sleep. But as soon as I breathed in the salty air, I felt better.

Jack was waiting for me with a smug look on his face. "Hey there, Papa."

Glaring at him, I growled, "Shut it."

We rode back to the Grand mostly in silence, the breeze cleansing me.

"I need to buy a car and maybe rent a house for the next six months. Something both Shell and her daughter can visit and will have space," I told Jack when we rolled up in front of the resort. Then I pulled out a few hundred dollars and asked him if he could help with some of the legwork.

"For you to have a happy ending, I would have done it for free," he had the nerve to say, and I grinned at him.

"Wait here. I'm going to see her," I said before jumping out and heading toward reception.

I doubted my room was ready, but I could leave my luggage and get right over to Shell. I'd texted when I landed and said I wasn't waiting to see her. She was at the coffee shop and told me her parents knew. Maybe she thought this would scare me off, but I was a big boy.

Back in the Jeep, Jack took me to Island Coffee and said he'd be outside making some calls for me.

"Morning," I said as I walked in the door, catching Sam and Shell hovering over something on the counter.

As soon as she saw me, Shell snatched up the papers and tossed them under the counter. If she thought she was being slick, she wasn't.

"Morning," Sam said sternly to me.

"Hi," I said to Shell, letting her dad know he wasn't intimidating me.

"Can I get you a coffee?" she asked me, like I was a regular Joe and not the father of her unborn child. No way was she going to treat me like I was any customer.

"Your dad can. I want to see you." I looked at Sam and said, "Half-and-half."

"Come here," I said to Shell, and she came around the counter. Her white shirt clung to her small belly, and I had to grip the counter at the sight of it.

"You okay?" Her palm came to rest on my forearm.

I nodded.

"Shit just got real." I felt Sam eyeing me, so I added, "Nothing I can't handle." Rescuing my manhood, I pulled Shell in for an embrace.

I inhaled her scent like a drug as I held her close. I wasn't sure why, but my world seemed to settle when I had her in my arms. Paying no mind to her dad, I slid my hand down her side and between us to touch her belly.

"How's our little guy?" I whispered. It was as if aliens had inhabited my body, but it felt good. I wasn't opposed to them staying.

A smack on my arm knocked me out of my thoughts. "Cal, stop saying that. What if I have a girl? Will you be disappointed?"

"No."

"Here you go, Caleb," Sam said, interrupting. "What do you think about you and your brother expecting babies at the same time?"

"Uh," I looked to Shell, and she nodded.

"We all know," she said softly.

"I'm sure it will be cool." What else could I say? I had no clue.

Giving me a pointed look, Sam said, "Your brother went about things the usual way. Got married, then started a family."

I nodded. All of a sudden, it was boiling hot in the coffee shop. My track pants hugged my balls like a vise—or was that Sam?

"My brother is a better man than me. I know that."

Shell glared at Sam. "Dad, please."

"What? This man needs to decide what he wants. Does he want you or to play games?"

I didn't know what I wanted, but no one threw down the gauntlet when it came to me.

"I do know what I want, sir. A healthy baby, your daughter to take care of herself and be happy, and I don't want to upset Weezie—ever."

It was the truth. I might not have ever verbalized it before, but it was.

"Then do it," Sam said and walked to the back.

"Sorry about that," Shell said, still standing in front of me.

"Don't be." My palm cupped her cheek. "He has every right to question me. But right now, I'm going to kiss you. I can't wait."

Leaning closer, I felt my heart beat faster as our lips met. At first, it was soft, then not. If we weren't in public and inside the coffee shop her dad owned, I might have fucked her right on the counter.

Instead, my hand found her belly again. "You look beautiful. I keep meaning to ask, but have you been sick? Maybe that's why you're not gaining weight."

Shell shook her head. "No. I didn't have morning sickness with Weez either. As for me, I look pregnant, and I'm only going to get bigger."

"Good. That means you're taking care of yourself."

"Drink your coffee," she said, changing the subject, nodding toward the counter where my cup waited for me.

I reached for it and took a sip, letting the caffeine spread through my veins. "Jack is outside. I'm going to rent a house here for the next few months with space for you and Weezie to spend time there. I'm going to be here as much as I can to take care of you."

"Cal."

"Don't *Cal* me. It's done." When Shell put a hand on her hip and was about to argue, I said, "Now show me the secret papers under the counter."

This made her eyes sparkle and shoot fire at the same time. I'd touched a nerve, and I loved it.

"Later. I need to take some beans to the Ritz, and then pick up Weez. It's a half day for her at school."

"Oh, good. You can bring her to the hotel, and she can swim."

Shell frowned. "I don't know."

Getting close, tucking her hair behind her ear, I said, "We're having a baby, and I hear Weezie is happy about it. I want to have her to the hotel, spoil her, let her know I'm here for her."

"There's that whiplash again."

After sucking on Shell's earlobe a few seconds, I broke free and whispered, "Nah. This is what I want, and we're doing it."

I had no idea how I was going to pull this off—be a dad, a giving partner, cool to Weezie, and work. But I'd make it happen.

# CHAPTER NINETEEN

*Shell*

After I made sure Weezie buckled herself in the backseat, I drove off from school, willing my hands not to shake.

Weezie missed her dad, but was also angry with him. She blamed herself for his leaving. I knew this because she told me a few times, and I did everything I could to discourage this line of thinking.

Then she'd spent time with Adam and Rylan, and fell in love with everything that was them. They were all I heard about from her, things like, "Rylan said Adam is bringing her coffee," and "Adam carried me to bed," and "Did you know Adam may get a puppy?"

In her mind, she dreamed of an Adam for me . . . and now Cal showed up again.

"Mommy, can we go to the park?" Weezie asked, and this time, I had one better for her.

"Remember Cal?"

She nodded. Of course she did. "Your special friend? My baby's daddy?"

I had done my best to explain that Cal had been a special friend, and we cared so much for each other that we created a baby. When I thought about it, it sounded like a crock of shit, but I didn't know how else to explain my situation.

Even with his newfound caretaking gig and renting a house, Cal wasn't marrying me. He was easing his own guilt and satisfying his curiosity, and probably wanting to keep the booty-call connection open. Which in a lot of ways didn't bother me, because it wasn't like I was going to date and get some with two kids at home.

"Yes," I told Weezie. "He's visiting and staying at the Grand, and he invited us swimming."

Luckily, I was prepared for a reaction of mammoth proportions from Weezie, because she started hooting and hollering in the backseat.

"Did you bring my suit?"

I nodded.

"Yay! Can I get chicken tenders?"

The frugal single mom in me wanted to say we'd see, but I knew Cal would charge the entire pool menu to his room if she wanted.

"Sure can," I said, wondering who the hell I was these days.

"See? I can swim," Weezie later called to Cal from the pool.

He was sitting on the edge drinking an iced tea, watching her after ordering me to sit in the lounge chair. That was after the chicken fingers for Weezie and the grilled chicken salad and fries for me. Cal watched me eat every bite over his fish tacos from the other chaise in the cabana.

Of course he'd rented one, complete with a TV so Weezie could watch a show from her towel on the grass while sucking down a Shirley Temple. If she had stars in her eyes when it came to Adam, then Cal could hang the moon. He didn't take his attention away from my daughter in the pool, his attention solely on her.

My gaze, however, was focused on his muscular back and the lines where it met his board shorts. Pregnancy hormones still had a hold on my libido. Thank God for Weezie, or we'd be back in his room already, the whole resort gossiping about us.

Cal got Weezie's attention. "Hey, want to take a break?"

"Can I get ice cream?" my daughter, the opportunist, asked.

He nodded and walked her over to the bar where he grabbed a towel and wrapped her up before setting her on a stool where Teddi fawned all over her.

Next thing I knew, Cal approached without Weezie. "Theodora is going to get her a sundae and keep an eye on her. Is that okay?"

I wanted to argue, but I didn't. "Thanks. She's having the best day of her life, it seems."

"Who wouldn't here at the Grand?" Cal sat at the end of my lounger, rubbing my foot. "Are you good? What can I get you?"

Weezie had watched with big eyes as he kissed my cheek hello when we arrived. She'd be doing backflips over the foot rub, but I couldn't bring myself to tell him to stop.

"Jack called when you were on your way over," Cal said. "I'm going to see two houses tomorrow. I'd like you to come with me."

Swallowing, I said, "I can't. I'm working a double at Camila's."

"Shell. I don't like it."

"This is how I make a living, Cal. I'm working on some other options, but until they come together, this is what I have."

His palm worked its way up my leg and back down again, massaging my sore calf. "I want to know what you're working on. And before I forget, your belly looks amazing in that suit."

I burst out laughing. "It looks like a bowling ball."

This made him laugh too. "Don't talk about my son that way."

"Oh. My. God."

"Shush," he said. "Now tell me before your daughter comes back over. She doesn't like my attention diverted, and that's a damn good thing. Because the things I want to do to you have no place out here."

Rolling my eyes, I took a sip of my water but didn't respond.

"Go on. Tell me," he said.

The stubborn man wasn't going to let it go, so I took a chance.

"I'm working on syrups. For coffee."

"And? What's your pitch?" His attention wholly focused on me, Cal made me feel like the sun rose and set on my ideas. Not once had I ever felt that way with Ricky.

"Well, I get asked a lot about flavored beans, but my dad is a purist, and that was going to be a solid no from him. But then I thought about island-flavored syrups for coffee drinks or hot cocoas or whatever, locally sourced and manufactured. I perfected my simple syrup, and then I started playing with various extracts. The problem is I have to rent space to make it and bottle it to sell it commercially. Those are the numbers I'm crunching."

"Who's making the packaging?" Cal asked, not missing a beat.

"I have that solved. I found a glass bottle manufacturer, and Brianna helped me design a label. She went to school for a semester of graphic design before quitting."

"Does Adam know all this?"

I nodded.

Cal frowned, grumbling, "Fucker."

"I asked him not to tell you. I feel like he shouldn't be in the middle of us."

"How much is the manufacturing?"

"It's complicated, a sliding-scale thing. It goes down the more I make. I could start bottling it on my own, but this is the preferred way."

"I'll back it."

"This is why I didn't want to tell you. I need to figure this out."

"Why? You're having my baby."

"Our baby," I said firmly.

"Our baby. I want to back your business. I want you done with waiting tables. You can pay me back when you make money."

"Cal—"

"No. No Cal. I told you that once already today. Now, moving on. I want to see these houses tomorrow, and then I want to hear the baby again and take you to dinner. Weezie too, but if you can break free, I'd like a date."

"I'm not your employee," I said with a touch of snark. "I get that this is all new to you, but I'm my own person. I appreciate the offer of the money, and we can sit down with Adam and discuss it because he wants to fund it too."

"Adam isn't funding it," I said, but left it there, deciding to leave that one alone.

Shell's expression softened. "I'm going to work tomorrow, and then we can have dinner the next day. The two of us. So, I'm compromising. As for the doctor, you'll have to wait. I have my big ultrasound in a month."

I watched him swallow, his Adam's apple bobbing up and down. Cal wasn't used to being bossed around, but this wasn't his show to direct.

"When is that?"

"My appointment is May twentieth, and the ultrasound is set for June third."

He couldn't answer right away because Weezie made her way back to us. I glanced over to see Teddi watching her walk all the way. I waved and Teddi blew a kiss my way—surely some secret signal I didn't get.

"Mom! I had s'mores ice cream with chocolate sauce."

"Mmm, sounds delish. Now you have to wait to swim again."

Weezie's face fell. "I know. Can I watch a show?"

I wanted to tell her we would go play on the beach in the sand, but Cal was already wielding the remote, and I tossed out any ideas that he wasn't directing this show. He was.

He confirmed this as soon as Weezie was situated. "We'll eat at the Ritz this time, and I'll make sure to be here for those appointments. I'll be in my house, and you'll be able to go over all the bottling information with me."

Rather than respond, I went back to my romance novel and sparkling water.

What was the use in resisting?

# CHAPTER TWENTY

## Cal

Yesterday, after another long run, I'd spent the morning in my room working. A number of clients were ready to sign, and I needed to tidy up some details. Then I called Adam and let him know I'd be funding the syrups. He argued with me, and I kept insisting it was my responsibility, but eventually, we came to the conclusion that it was a family thing, so I gave in.

My brother went on a long rant about trust and relationships and not keeping secrets. Then I moaned about the doctor appointments, and he agreed waiting was a pain, but the women's bodies were theirs and we had to abide by their wishes.

I hated when he was right . . . especially when he said I needed to tell Mom I was becoming a father.

When he and Rylan had shared their news, Mom was especially excited. I had yet to tell her for so many reasons. First, she'd insist that Shell and I get married, and then she'd complain I wasn't marrying a Jewish girl.

It had been a shitty morning made shittier when I manned up and called Mom, and she accused me of ruining her happiness when it came to Adam.

Like Shell's mom, she mentioned doing things in the natural order—marriage, then babies.

Why was everyone so hung up on that? Didn't she realize Rylan had been pregnant at the wedding? Not to mention, Shell didn't seem to want to marry me.

Despite all the craziness, I'd thought about going to see Shell for lunch at Camila's. But I knew if I did, I'd go back for dinner, and my stalker tendencies were wearing thin when it came to her. Instead, I found myself wandering the jewelry store in the hotel, intentionally ignoring the engagement ring section.

Looking at rental houses had consumed that afternoon. I'd settled on a four-bedroom place with its own pool. Much later, when I showed up at Camila's for my dinner, I'd share the news and come bearing gifts . . . the matching necklace to the anklet for Shell, and a bangle bracelet for Weezie.

I waited until the end of the night to give them to Shell, and while she said it was too much, I noted a shadow of disappointment cross her face.

Did she think I was going to propose? While she was still waiting tables?

She allowed me to drive her home in her car, Jack following, and gave me a chaste kiss at the door before heading inside to relieve her mom. I got the feeling she wasn't in the mood for me to interact with her.

Which brought me to now, another morning of work, and pissed that I hadn't seen Shell yet. Deciding it was time for her to be with me, I called her.

"Hello? Caleb?" she said when she answered her phone.

"Yes, it's me." *Who the fuck else would it be*, I thought, but I didn't ask the second part.

"Everything okay?" she asked.

"No."

"What happened?" I could hear the panic in her voice. Shell was made to nurture.

"Nothing. I want to see you, that's all. I've been here two days and have barely seen you."

"Oh. I'm making some syrups. Experimenting."

"Where?"

"My kitchen."

"I'll be right there."

"Cal—"

I hung up before she could argue.

I texted Jack, who was still driving me because I was trying to lease an Audi. I was allowed to drive for six months in the Caymans with my license from the States, but after that, I'd have to take a test. In the meantime, the dealership didn't want to lease me the car.

Arriving at Shell's, I told Jack to go about his day. I was going to be a while.

Knocking on the door, I was greeted by Shell in an apron, her hair in a bun on top of her head. I wanted to let her hair down and have my way with her right there, but I didn't.

She gave me a smile. "Hi."

"Hi, you," I said as I crossed the threshold. I didn't wait before gathering her close for a kiss. "You taste like coconut."

She licked her lips, and I decided to apply for that job.

"I'm working on a coconut syrup right now. It's why I've been picking up doubles at Camila's. So I can do this." When I opened my mouth to speak, she held a hand in the air. "Not now with the quitting."

I decided it was in my best interest not to argue. "Let me taste," I said instead.

She led me to the kitchen. It was a wreck, bowls and ingredients everywhere. "I got carried away with tweaking a cinnamon-vanilla variety first," she said with a shrug.

I tried to imagine if my place had ever looked like this, and decided it hadn't.

"That's why they invented cleaning up," Shell said before spooning some syrup from a dish and bringing the spoon to my mouth.

I hardened in certain places while softened in others, like my heart.

My mouth opened, and Shell dropped a small amount of the syrup on my tongue. A moan came unbidden. "I don't have a sweet tooth, but that is some amazing shit."

A smile formed on Shell's face, and I noticed she was wearing the necklace under the apron. I stepped closer and sneaked another lick off the spoon before taking it from her and setting it on the counter.

"I like this," I said, tucking my index finger under the seashell-lined chain.

"I don't have anywhere nice enough to wear it, so I put it on to cook." A small laugh escaped her, and I kissed it away.

"You can wear it tonight. To dinner." I ran my lips over her cheek and back to her mouth.

"Cal, wait," she mumbled, and I stepped back.

"I . . . I . . . I'm confused. You're hot, then cold, then hot again. Me, I'm hot all the time for you. I shouldn't admit that, but I am. I don't know what to think."

Gathering her close with her small belly between us, I said, "Shell, I'm hot as hell for you. All the fucking time. I'm so hot, I don't know how to handle it, so I pretend to be cold. I'm here for you. All of me for all of you. I want to be good to you and Weez and our son . . . or daughter. I need to get on your dad's good side, and your mom's. My mom's too. Until then and after, I'm all about you."

A tear seemed to form in Shell's eye, but she blinked it away. "What's wrong with your mom? I didn't even meet her at the wedding. She was too caught up in everything else."

"She thinks we should be married," I said. "Just like your dad."

Shell broke free from my hold and turned around. I took the opportunity to ogle her muscular calves and the short shorts that covered her ass, a white T-shirt above.

"Do you want that? To get married, I mean." I didn't set out to ask, but it was starting to feel like I might want it. I had no clue.

She shook her head.

"Please turn back," I said. She did, and this time there definitely was a tear in her eye.

"I don't want to force another man to marry me," she choked out.

"Come here," I asked, and she did.

Holding her in my arms, I kissed the top of her forehead.

"No one forces me to do anything, Shell. Understand that. I want you, and I'm going to do you proud," I said, but left it at that. I needed to think this shit through.

Shell needed to believe I wasn't being coerced, and so did I.

We began to kiss. I didn't know who started it, but I was going to finish it.

My tongue entered her mouth, stroking hers, as I lifted her up and her legs wrapped around my waist. I set her ass on the counter and continued to kiss her as I untied her apron, tugging it off. Next came her T-shirt, and then I laid her back.

Sugars and spoons and little ramekins were scattered all around her. I found the spoon she'd fed me with and used it to drizzle some syrup down her belly. Bringing my head down over her, I licked it off, pleased to see goose bumps following in my path.

"I really like my island girl syrup," I mumbled as I gently kissed her belly.

I found myself at her shorts and yanked them down, revealing the prettiest pair of yellow bikini underwear. I loved that she didn't wear a tiny G-string but something that left a bit more to the imagination.

Yellow was certainly my girl's color.

Pushing the underwear to the side, I found the landing strip I'd been searching for. I didn't need anyone to direct me home.

A growl erupted from me as I drizzled some more syrup on Shell and leaned forward to lap it up. She moaned in earnest and didn't seem one bit fazed that she was naked in her kitchen. I guessed that since none of what she was making was for sale or commercial use, then the health department would have no problem with me ravaging her on her kitchen counter.

When Shell's back was arching off the counter and tiny quakes racked her body, I asked, "Do you want me?"

She nodded.

"Let me hear you say it."

"I want you. I want all of you, Cal."

Hearing that, I couldn't shove my pants down fast enough.

Seconds later, I was inside her, supporting her back with one arm and bracing myself with the other. It wasn't until we were both coming down from the haze that we looked around and burst out laughing.

"I'd better get this cleaned up before Weezie sees. She'll get ideas about making a mess."

"Can I say these are not ideas I want her to have?"

This only made Shell laugh harder.

"Here," I said, lifting her off the counter. "Why don't you go get cleaned up, and I'll start in here."

She opened her mouth to argue, but I shook my head.

"The sooner we clean up, the sooner you can pick up Weezie. And then later, we'll have our date."

I didn't know when I became a romantic, but it felt pretty damn good.

# CHAPTER TWENTY-ONE

• June •

*Shell*

"**M**om, I'm fine," I said, arguing with her while Weezie was upstairs playing with her new doll, courtesy of Cal.

"Shell, baby doll." My mother might have said my name sweetly, but the look on her face was anything but. "You're out of your league. Ricky was a nobody. You thought you loved him—I get that. But he did you dirty."

"Mom—"

When I started to speak, she raised a hand in the air to interrupt me. "I like Adam, but Caleb isn't Adam."

She'd started calling Cal by his full name after his last visit. Unfortunately, she'd shown up at the same time as he did to pick up Weezie. He'd come with Jack to pick me up for dinner, flashing his Rolex and white smile, picking Weezie up and spinning her in the air.

My mom was less than impressed with his antics, and even less so with his idea to rent a house on the island. *Temporarily*, she'd said, throwing his word back at him. Of course, Cal being the smooth businessman he was, he pretended like she wasn't having an attitude and entertained nonstop questions from Weezie.

"He's only getting a place here while you're pregnant. Then what? Does he want a family? Is he going to take care of you with all that money of his?"

I closed my eyes and ran my hand along my belly.

"Sit down," my mom barked.

Seated on a stool at the same counter where Cal and I had made love, had sex, or whatever it was, I took a breath.

"Look, Mom, I'm perfectly capable of taking care of myself. I'm starting production on the syrups in a few weeks, and I'm going full-time with Dad. Cal is planning to cover the cost of a sitter for the baby when he or she arrives."

Another new development was that Cal and I spoke on the phone about every other day. It usually evolved into a FaceTime where he talked to my belly. In these calls, I saw a softer side of him. Maybe it was the protective layer of technology that allowed him to be himself and let his guard down.

He'd often say hi to Weezie, asking her about school. It was during one of these calls that she'd mentioned American Girl dolls. She'd seen one at school that a friend had gotten on a trip to New York. Later that week, a doll arrived for her. Well, not only a doll, but a lot of furniture and outfits for the doll too.

Which brought me to now . . . my mom in my kitchen, Weezie soaking up every second with her doll, and Cal arriving in the morning.

"Don't stay in that house with him, Shell. Don't take my granddaughter and stay there. He'll never commit. Good you're working with your dad and Cal is paying up, but he's not Ricky. There's more he can do."

"Cal is doing enough," I shot back. "You know he and Adam are putting up the money for the syrups. I'm going to pay them back."

Mom shook her head with a tsk-tsk. "I don't know what's wrong with you. Did you hit your head? This man is the father of your baby. You don't need to pay him back."

"Enough," I said, standing to get a drink.

Then I braved the waters without a life preserver. "He's having a barbecue on Friday at his place, and he wants you and Dad there. He wants it to be a family thing."

"That man," Mom muttered, shaking her head. Walking out of the kitchen, she called out, "Come say 'bye to *Abuela*, Weezie."

My daughter, the sweet girl she was, did as she was told, and I was left alone with my thoughts.

*Landed.*

Cal texted me around ten o'clock just as I was finishing with a customer at the coffee shop. I'd started taking over the mid-morning to late-afternoon shift after I quit the restaurant. It let me chat with customers, feel them out on the syrups, and offer them samples.

*I can leave in a few to get you.*

After I texted him back, I went toward the rear of the shop and got my dad. He'd agreed to work for me today, so I could pick up Cal. Dad was softer than Mom to the idea of Cal in my life in whatever way he wanted to be.

"Are you happy, Shell?" my dad asked me as he wound his way up front behind me.

Untying my apron, taking a look at the bulge in my stomach, I said, "Yes. I'm doing something cool for me, and Cal is a good man. He may not be my husband, but he won't desert this baby."

I believed it, and for some reason, I was at peace with it.

When I arrived at the airport, I saw Cal standing outside, shades protecting his eyes from the punishing Caribbean sun, wearing khakis and a golf shirt, his suitcase next to him. I pulled up next to him, and he walked over and opened the driver's door. Without a word, he waited for me to get out so he could drive.

"Good to see you too," I said, trying to hide my smile.

"It will be better by my pool with you relaxing."

"I have to work some. My dad can't take all my shifts."

"The ultrasound is still tomorrow? At two?"

I nodded. The big day was finally here. The plan had been for Cal to come today and be here through next Tuesday. He'd asked for some time with me, a date night—he always won that battle—and a night for only Weezie and me. Then there was the family dinner and the ultrasound.

It was a nice break from the monotony of my life, and probably a big difference from the pace he kept in the city.

"Can't wait to christen the house," Cal said with a wink as he pulled out of the airport.

I almost made a comment on my larger appearance, but there was nothing I could do about it. I was just about halfway on this adventure.

"Open my messenger bag," Cal said while driving toward the West Bay.

"Me?"

"Who else is in the car?"

I did as I was told and found a copy of *What to Expect When You're Expecting*. This sent me into a fit of laughter.

"You think that's funny?" Cal said with a big smile. "I'm learning all about this shit."

"I can see that. You're going to be an expert," I teased.

"Maybe not an expert, but a heck of a dad."

There was no fitting answer to that comment. I knew he'd be a heck of a part-time dad, but not a full-time one, let alone a partner.

"How's your latest client?" I asked, changing the subject.

"Happy. He got to keep his house in Barbados, and she got the place in the Hamptons."

He hadn't used names, but I knew this was a celebrity chef. The client was mostly concerned with his properties, and I guessed Cal went to war for him, despite rumors of a girlfriend on the side. It wasn't hard to figure out who the chef was. *Internet, duh.*

We rode a while longer, listening to music and Cal asking about Weezie, until we pulled up at the house. I'd seen it when he first looked at it, but its enormity still shocked me. It was a giant white Tudor in the middle of a beach neighborhood. Gaudy, out-of-place columns stood in front of a red door.

"Come on." Cal jumped out of the car and rounded the hood. Leading me up the steps by my hand and unlocking the door, he smiled. "Welcome to my new pad."

I rolled my eyes.

"What?"

"You couldn't get less beachy than this," I said, taking in the marble floor and dramatic staircase for the second time. "It's an American mansion."

"I know, but it has a lot of amenities and more space than the villa at the Grand. I do miss those open-air pathways and the windows there, though."

Here, the air conditioning was blowing throughout the house. You could feel the cool breeze from the vents.

"Let's go see if they stocked the kitchen as promised." He headed toward the back. The layout was similar to Adam and Rylan's, but their house was a beachy contemporary.

"Should I take off my shoes?"

Cal turned and stared at me. "Do whatever you want, Shell. This is as much your space as mine."

He kept moving, but I was stuck standing in the foyer, freezing from the air-conditioning despite being pregnant.

"Shell, what's wrong?" He came back around to find me.

"This isn't my space," I said, staring at the marble floor. "My space is the tiny house I live in with Weez, and soon, our baby. It's dilapidated and run-down, but mine. Thank God, I never put Ricky's name on the deed since he wasn't paying any money toward it and my parents paid the down payment as a wedding gift. At the time, I thought they were stupid for doing so. I mean, Ricky and I were going to buy a house on our own."

Cal came close and wrapped an arm around me, putting his finger over my lips and whispering, "Shush."

I took a deep breath and realized he was right. I was rambling about things that had no significance between us.

"They do," he said.

"Was I talking out loud?"

He nodded, not letting go of me. "You're getting yourself upset. That's why I said to shush. The baby doesn't need you to be upset."

This time, it was my turn to nod.

"I want you to feel at home here," he said.

"I'm a guest."

"You're not," he said firmly.

I broke free from his embrace. "Cal, this house is bigger than my house and my parents' combined. I worked for tips until a week ago. I barely have any savings. I am most certainly a guest in a place like this, and often an employee."

He stood there perfectly still, just staring at me. I was getting myself upset again, and I didn't care.

"We're not moving in together," I said, just getting wound up. "We're not making a life together, outside of the baby and this *friends with benefits* thing we have going on. I know my place."

There was never a good time to discuss *what are we doing?* Yet, here we were doing it.

"That isn't your place, as a guest or employee." Cal approached again, tugging me to his chest, tipping my gaze toward his, his index finger on my chin. "I haven't given you a ring, but that doesn't mean this isn't something. We aren't *friends with benefits*. We're more. I'm doing right by you, and this is as much your space as mine. I don't live here. I make a living in New York, but when I'm here, you can be here, and when I'm not here, you can be here too."

I nodded. Cal hadn't made a promise to marry me or move here, but he was trying, I guessed. Although, he hadn't invited me to his home in New York, which made my mind wander.

Did he have someone else who shared that space? Was Sophia back in his life?

I told myself it wasn't my business. I didn't have the answers, nor could I find the words, so I kissed him. Why did I kiss him? It was complicated, but whatever we did have was the only thing I had, and I liked it.

Apparently, that kiss was enough of a response for Cal because he led me toward the kitchen and opened the fridge.

"What can I get you to drink?" he asked after making it known he wasn't going to marry me.

I mean, I knew that, but that didn't make it hurt any less.

"Water," I said, taking in the man in front of me.

His hair was a bit disheveled from his flight, and his shirt a little wrinkled, but his eyes were bright and promising. I realized then that I was falling for him.

He brought over a glass and a liter of bottled water, then poured it for me. Once I'd taken a sip, he took my glass and set it down, standing in front of the stool where I was sitting.

"Shell, I didn't say I wasn't going to give you a ring. I said I haven't. What I meant was I haven't *yet*."

I swallowed my words, afraid of what I might say next. Crazy thoughts were tumbling around in my head like clothes in a dryer.

Cal turned and paced the kitchen. "I don't know what I'm doing, that's for sure. The only thing I don't want to do is hurt you. I'm trying."

His words trailed off at the end, and in that pause, I felt for Cal. He was trying, so I stood and went to him. This time it was me pulling him close and kissing away his fear.

We stayed like that for a while, our lips locked, our arms around each other, the world and all its responsibilities slipping away. For this one moment in time, it was what we both needed, and we didn't need to speak it aloud.

# CHAPTER TWENTY-TWO

After the episode in my kitchen, I was left completely drained.

All this relationship shit was harder than I ever thought it would be, which was why I'd avoided it in the first place. I'd thought it was difficult, and it was. I wanted to punch the wall or go for a run. Instead, I could only try deep breathing to calm myself for the woman carrying my child.

After exploring the house and then sitting outside with me for a while, Shell had to go. She needed to make some deliveries for the coffee shop and do some paperwork before picking up Weezie.

I asked if she wanted to get dinner, and she said Weezie had a playdate and she didn't have the heart to cancel. Since I had no clue what a playdate was, I couldn't argue. Later last night, I searched for it in my book, but I guessed it was something that came well after the birth since it wasn't in the what-to-expect book.

*Fuck,* I'd need a new book on what to expect when you inherited a kid.

Now, I was finally in my goddamn car I'd been trying to buy for weeks, and picking up Shell for the ultrasound. She texted she'd be at the coffee shop, so I went a few minutes early to grab a cup and make nice with her dad. I knew how this shit went . . . I needed to keep showing up, so they didn't think I was going to disappear. I'd seen it enough in my clients.

"Morning," I said to Sam, who was finishing up with a customer.

As soon as he gave them their change, he asked me, "Coffee?"

I nodded.

"With Shell's syrup?" I didn't care for sweetened coffee, but I wasn't going to turn down her dad when he was offering his daughter's products. "For sure."

"Coconut or vanilla?"

"Oh, I have a choice? Coconut. When in Rome," I said, trying to joke, but Sam didn't laugh.

He poured my coffee, added the syrup and half-and-half, and handed me a cup. "On the house."

I shook my head. "No, I don't want to do that."

"Drink your coffee and shut up. You and your brother are bankrolling this whole project. I'll give you a coffee when I want."

When his dark eyes narrowed on me, I decided not to argue. Instead, I drank my coffee.

"Wow, this is great. Doesn't taste fake or have that aftertaste."

Sam nodded, seeming to know what I meant.

Thankfully, Shell came out of the back and smiled. "Hey."

"This is fucking great." I tipped my cup toward her. "Coconut."

Her face lit up with pride. "Thank you."

"Later, you'll have to show me how you do it. I do remember seeing you practicing, and it was messy, but I loved it."

She pressed her lips together, a nonverbal warning to not say any more about our kitchen tryst.

Smart enough to read the signals, I said, "Let's go see our baby."

"Call me later," Sam said. "We'll have Weez, and she'll want to know."

"Yep," Shell said, walking toward the door in black leggings and a long white off-the-shoulder sweater, both hugging her ass.

Other than kissing, we hadn't been intimate since I'd arrived this time, and I was wondering when that might happen. Again, though, smart enough not to ask.

Outside, she said, "Did Jack bring you?"

"Got my car," I said with a wink.

"Let me guess? A two-seater Jeep?"

"Have a little more confidence in me." I took her hand and walked her over to my silver Audi crossover wagon. Beeping the locks and opening the passenger door, I said, "Safety first."

Shell's mouth opened, but then she snapped it shut and slid into the car.

"Everything looks good," the technician said, rolling a jelly-covered wand over Shell's small belly.

We'd seen the heart beating on the screen and what looked like our baby sucking its thumb. Shell swiped at her eye twice, and I could tell she was fighting tears.

Me? I was fighting an anxiety attack. At least I knew that type of thing did nobody good in this moment. Back to deep breathing, I sat next to Shell, holding her hand as we watched our little alien on the screen.

"Would you like to know the sex?" the tech asked.

Shell looked over to me. Like I said, I was seated next to her, holding her hand like this was normal for me, but it wasn't.

"Do you?" I asked.

She nodded. "I didn't know with Weez, and it made it seem so long until the birth."

"Let's have it," I said to the tech, flashing a smile like I thought I should. What the fuck did I know?

"It's a boy!" the munchkin of a technician exclaimed.

Sure enough, the little arrow on the screen was pointing toward his tiny dick. I stared at it, knowing it was going to be a great one, but even more so, he was going to be a wonderful boy and then man.

"Told you," I said to Shell.

Twisting her lips, she gently smacked my arm. "Beginner's luck."

"Ha. My son. Our son."

Suddenly, my cheeks hurt, and I realized they hadn't felt that way since I settled my first divorce case. I was smiling for real.

"Okay, that's all for me," the tech whispered, sensing Shell and I were having a moment. On her way out, she took a few snapshots out of the printer and left them on the counter by the door.

"You good?" I asked when Shell and I were alone.

She nodded. "I am, are you? Can you believe it . . . a boy?"

"A boy," I said reverently, repeating her words.

"I was hoping we could name our baby for your sister." Shell spoke quietly, looking away from me. "I didn't know her, and we don't talk much about it, but I also know a little from Rylan. She was the B to Adam's A and your C."

Emotion clogged my throat in a way I didn't know possible. "That's the nicest thing anyone has ever wanted to do for me. Her name was Becca. She was the B in the middle of us, and the best of all three of us. I'd like that very much . . . for her to have a namesake."

"Do we use the first initial?" Shell asked.

"That's the tradition. There are a lot of B names for boys. We can look up some together."

It occurred to me how happy this would make my mom, but I didn't voice the thought. I knew better than to take away from this moment between just the two of us.

"That would be nice," Shell said before she used her gown to wipe away the excess jelly on her stomach.

I held out my hand and helped her stand. As she started to get dressed, I went to see the printouts. My index finger traced the tiny baby while I held the picture in my other hand.

"We made him," I said to myself. Then I whispered, "I promise to be there for you, buddy. I hated not having a dad."

When I lifted my head, Shell was quietly watching me.

"Ready?" I asked, not wanting to discuss the emotions flaring up inside me.

"We have to call Weez."

"As soon as we get in the car."

Shell shook her head. "No, she won't be home yet. Soon."

We walked out of the exam room together, and Shell thanked the staff as we exited the office.

"Since Weez is still tied up, can we celebrate?" I asked. "Go to a late lunch?" I was hopeful Shell wouldn't blow me off again.

"That sounds great. I'm starving, actually."

I wanted to fist-pump the air, but chose to put my arm around Shell and hold her close instead. "Where would you like to eat? Want to go to the Grand? I kind of miss it."

"Sure. I can tell Teddi when we're there. Oh, I need to call Rylan. I guess you'll tell Adam. They'll know soon too. What they're having, I mean," Shell said, rambling and seeming genuinely happy.

"I'll call Adam in a few. He wanted to know. It feels weird that they're not here, but I know he's showing her around Michigan."

"I'm sure she's glad it's not snowing."

"I'll bet. She said it's not her thing."

Shell looked out the window, her voice wistful as she said, "I'd like to see it once."

I made note of this, but had no idea what it would take to get her to visit me. Would she come with Weezie or not? Or with our baby?

# CHAPTER TWENTY-THREE

*Shell*

"Table for two," Cal told the hostess at Eye of the Sea. I'd suggested eating by the pool, but Cal wanted to come here. I'd never been to such a fancy lunch. I tried to argue, but he wouldn't hear of it.

"Right this way," the hostess said. She was new, and I hadn't met her before. Rylan had been helping management to find some new staff while she was in the States, so maybe she'd hired the new girl.

Seated by the window, Cal and I watched as the ocean lapped in the distance. The summer's approaching humidity hung in the air outside, and I was grateful for a seat in the air-conditioning.

"Are you disappointed?" Cal asked out of nowhere. "Did you want another girl?"

"No, of course not. I want a healthy baby is all. Well, I didn't even know I wanted another baby."

Cal's brow furrowed, and I could tell he wasn't sure if I was serious or not.

"I'm joking," I told him, and his face relaxed. "I'm very excited to have a little boy. I know Weezie will be over the moon to have someone to boss around."

"She is a little bossy, I've noticed. Not in a bad way," Cal said quickly. "I wasn't trying to be mean. I meant she likes to tell me what to do, and I do it."

"I knew you didn't. The power of little girls. Works on mostly everyone except her dad. He didn't stick around."

Cal reached over the table and took my hand. "Hey, don't ruin today with that," he said softly.

I nodded and forced back whatever emotions were trying to surface.

We were still holding hands when the server came over and told us about the specials, one of which was a bacon cheeseburger with hand-cut fries. My mouth watered. It wasn't something I normally ate, but it sounded salty, cheesy, and just plain delicious.

"Your eyes lit up over that burger," Cal said after the server had taken our drink orders and hurried off.

"Was I that far gone for a cheeseburger?"

"Oh, you were."

I slipped my hand out from his to take a sip of my water, and as our hands separated, his pale compared to my brown, I thought about his mom and what she would think.

"Are you going to tell your mom we're having a boy?"

He shook his head. "Soon, not today."

"This baby will carry on the family name . . . at least, I assumed. Are you ashamed?"

"What?"

"Of me? Weez? Who I am?" Oh no. I was letting my hormones and feelings get the best of me.

"Shell, I'm not ashamed of you or tha you're having my baby. I'll admit, we got off to a strange start, but things feel like they're going to be fine. I would certainly hope my son will carry on my name."

I reminded myself that Cal was a lawyer. An absolute bullshitter, and I was falling for it.

"Well, you haven't told your mom yet, so it wasn't a big leap to make."

When Cal just took a swig of his water, I worried what that might mean. Nerves? Lying? I didn't know his tells yet.

"I was going to call her while you told Teddi, and then I thought we could call Rylan and Adam," he said, and when I didn't reply, he added, "I thought we'd enjoy this moment just the two of us."

My eyes widened. "Oh."

Luckily for me, the server came and took our order, and then it was only small talk until my decadent burger came, and I made love to the entire sandwich and fries with my mouth.

After a steady stream of phone calls to friends and family to share the news, we'd finally made it to Friday night dinner.

Adam and Rylan had been thrilled, but Cal's mom? I wasn't sure. Cal had said she was excited, but I was beginning to think guzzling water was a tell of his, because he'd downed a bottle while telling me. Weezie, of course, was ready to take on the little tyke in her army.

"Can I have one more soda, Mom?" Weezie yelled from the kitchen through the open doorway, rationalizing, "I'm the big sister."

I was busy setting the table outside, trying to still my nerves with mindless work.

We'd come to Cal's right after school, and unlike me, Weezie made herself right at home. She'd quickly changed and jumped into the pool before settling into the hot tub.

Cal said, "That's a better place for you," on her decision to sit in the jacuzzi.

"Why?" my daughter asked, of course.

"It's not too deep."

*Oh dear. Cal the nervous Nellie is back.*

"Would you like a soda?" he asked Weezie, and she's six, so that was a definite yes.

"Okay, come up and sit here on the side. With your feet in, but that's it," he told her, wrapping a towel around her shoulders. "I'll go get it, but don't move. Promise?"

Weezie nodded, and off he went to the kitchen. I'd watched all this from my chair in the shade where I was reviewing some contracts on my laptop—a new one courtesy of Adam.

Cal returned in record time, soda bottle and cup in hand.

"Oh, can I have the bottle?" Weezie exclaimed. She was wild for those glass bottles of Coca-Cola.

"Not by the pool. No glass."

I bit back a smile at that, wondering how Cal had turned so paternal so quickly for someone who hadn't wanted a family.

He made a fancy show of pouring the drink from high above the cup and presenting it to Weezie with a bow. I had work to do, but hadn't been able to tear my gaze away from the scene.

Weezie sipped her soda while Cal set the glass bottle on the table before returning next to her, dipping his legs into the jacuzzi too. He'd been wearing board shorts and a T-shirt when we arrived, ready to hang with Weezie, which was why he was taking a shower and changing right now while I fussed with the table.

I jumped when I heard his deep voice outside. "You don't have to do that. They can." He nodded his head toward the kitchen where an island catering staff prepped the barbecue.

"I do," I whispered.

"Mom, I'm staying here with the bottle," Weezie yelled from the couch.

She was never going to sleep later after all the sugar. For a quick second, I thought about suggesting we spend the night at Cal's. Maybe then he would second-guess all this shacking up when he was on the island.

"I like helping," I told him. "I've never had a party catered in all my life. Even my wedding, my mom and I did all the cooking for the reception."

Cal's face scrunched up, his brow furrowing.

Immediately, I said, "I'm sorry. I didn't mean to upset you."

He came closer. "You didn't. The deadbeat did." Cal's voice was low, his words meant for only me. "Now, let's go get you a water and you can sit down."

We didn't have a chance, because my parents walked right through the gate and into the backyard.

"We're here," my mom called out. "We figured it was out back," she said, her head on a swivel as she took in the place.

Without missing a beat, Cal said, "Perfect. Come on in and let me get you a drink."

My mom asked for a glass of wine. My dad opted for a Coke like Weezie, who had jumped off the couch and was chattering to him how he couldn't have the bottle outside.

Cal seemed to be taking it all in stride.

"Have a seat," he told my mom. "Inside, outside, wherever you're comfortable."

Mom sat down on an outside chair and looked at Weezie. "Baby girl, go put a coverup on. It's not polite to dance around in your swimsuit when we eat."

"But I want to go in the hot tub again, *Abuela*."

"Is she allowed?" My mom looked at me.

"There's no rules here, apparently," I whispered.

Mom sniffed. "Kids need rules."

My mom was a walking contradiction, a nonstop yin-yang of feelings and emotions and actions. Don't pay Cal back. Make Cal bend to your rules. Force Cal into commitment.

"It's okay, she's having fun," I said to my mom, and then told Weezie, "Ten minutes."

She nodded and walked-ran over to the hot tub.

Cal appeared with the drinks and hollered, "One sec," to Weezie.

"I'm fine," she hollered back.

I could see his struggle. He wanted to look after Weezie and be responsible, and he was, but he also didn't want to ignore my folks.

"It's okay, I'm right here." I sat down in a high-back chair facing the hot tub and kept an eye on Weezie.

A server came around with appetizers. Shrimp cocktail, conch fritters, and some type of burrata on toast adorned the tray.

I was about to select a piece, and Cal said from across the way, "Is burrata okay?"

"I'm having a shrimp." I waved the crustacean in the air, and he turned to talk with my dad. I heard snippets of their conversation, something about supply chain, shipping, and America.

I didn't even want to know.

We stayed like that for the allotted ten minutes I'd given to Weezie, and then I went to help her get dry and dressed.

By the time I was back, the grill was smoking, and someone was flipping steaks and burgers.

Weezie ran to my mom, cuddling with her before my mom said, "Soon, you'll have to share me."

"*Abuela*, that's okay. I'm getting big," my daughter said back.

"Unless you move to America, and then I won't have either of you."

Thank goodness I wasn't eating, or I would have choked. Suddenly, I was burning hot in my lightweight sweater and maternity jeans.

"Mom!"

"What? Adam moved here, and it's clear your guy has too much work in the Big Apple to do the same, so you can go there."

"Mom. Again, stop. I'm not moving. Cal isn't moving. He's not Adam."

"That's for sure," my mom muttered.

Cal shot her the side-eye at that but was too smart to engage. Not me, though.

Whipping my hair back, I said, "Mom, this is all we are, okay? Be happy."

The cook came out, unaware of the tension, and said, "Dinner is ready."

"Perfect." Cal stood and acted like he hadn't just been insulted.

I didn't think he appreciated the comparison to his brother. Cal wasn't like Adam, and he had no intention of being like him, despite his whole *I haven't given you a ring yet* speech.

"That was a disaster," I said to Cal after he buckled Weezie into the backseat and then opened the driver's door for me.

"At least your dad likes me."

"He's trying. You got me to quit the restaurant, so he's temporarily satisfied."

Cal leaned in and brushed his lips across my cheek. "Wish you'd stay."

"I can't. It's not the right look with Weez. She's young and doesn't understand what all this means."

He nodded and placed a quick kiss on my lips. "Tomorrow. Dinner at the Ritz. You and me. I want you all to myself for one night."

I confirmed and then got into my car and went home to my dilapidated shack, certain Weezie would dream of his mansion for months. Mentally, I beat myself up for even bringing her over.

But when I got home, the evening went even more downhill.

I didn't dream, let alone sleep, because something upset my stomach shortly after I lay down. I spent the night on the bathroom floor, finally calling my doctor at three o'clock in the morning. She said for me to come in for a quick check in the morning, sure that it was either a virus, something I ate, or second-trimester morning sickness.

By the morning, the sickness had abated, and I decided to not tell Cal. When it hit again as we were leaving for dinner, though, I had to come clean.

Cal and I never made it to the Ritz on our date. He looked so sad all dressed up in his navy dress shirt, chinos, and Ferragamo loafers, ready for a night out on the town . . . or the beach.

"I've never had a date cancel for this reason," he said sheepishly. "But it's okay. I want you to feel better."

I didn't know whether he meant it or not. A tiny red flag waved itself in my mind. What would he do when the baby was sick? Or Weezie?

Without the energy to bring any of this up, I lay on the couch with a bucket, and Cal sat in the chair, unsure of what to do. Weezie brought me water and ginger ale until my mom picked her up.

After what felt like an endless evening, I sent Cal home around ten, and he didn't argue.

The next morning, I woke up feeling fine, and Weezie begged to go to Cal's. She swam, and he did his best to be attentive to me, until dinnertime when another wave of sickness hit.

After another call to the doctor, we agreed it was nausea related to the hormone surge, combined with my prenatal vitamin. She recommended one with a time-release on the B vitamin. Cal filled it for me on Monday morning before he worked from his rental house.

All we had left was Monday night, and since the new vitamins hadn't kicked in yet, I spent it pretty much the same as I'd been spending my last few evenings.

Tuesday morning, I texted Cal to have a safe trip and we'd talk soon. I couldn't stand the idea of an in-person good-bye after what he'd seen and my state. It was obviously not a turn-on.

Cal was a good-time guy, not ready for this . . . whatever this was.

# CHAPTER TWENTY-FOUR

*Cal*

"You're an absolute fuckup," Adam said as he strolled into my office, then continued without allowing me to respond. "Wait. Haven't we had this talk before? Several times?"

"Nice to see you too, brother," I said. "Are you ready for lunch? Signed the NDA? This is a big one. You'll send your baby to college with this one."

We had a lunch meeting with a late-night TV host, a nice referral from the chef we'd worked with. This was a very nasty divorce in which the TV host was splitting from his wife of ten years for another celebrity. It was bound to be in every magazine and paper, drawing a lot of eyeballs. The fees would be generous.

"And your baby too," Adam said, leaning against my doorjamb. "Remember the little baby boy tucked inside a woman in the middle of the Cayman Islands? The same woman who you apparently told that you hadn't given her a ring to *yet*, and then mucked it all up by running the fuck out of there when she got sick."

"For fuck's sake, take a breath, bro." I leaned back in my chair and closed my eyes. Without looking at Adam, I asked, "How the hell do you know all that?"

"You see, ladies chat. Rylan called Shell to say congrats on having a boy and to see how she was feeling. By the way, we're having a girl. We found out yesterday. Anyway, Shell put on a tough voice and then apparently broke into tears and told the whole story to Ry. Of course, she made Ry swear not to mention it to me, but you know Rylan. Cal, your girl pretends to be detached, but she's anything but. She was wrecked over this. Bro, you've got to get your shit together. You're going to be a father."

As his words sank in, shame crept up my throat, clogging what I had to say. Finally, I choked out, "I don't know what that means to be a father. We grew up without one. You were all I had, and then you went on a rampage when Becca ended her life. I. Do. Not. Know. What. I'm. Doing."

Everyone thought Adam had taken our sister's death the worst. We were a freaking trio—triplets—and what was I supposed to do, carry on like normal? I worked, fucked, and partied, but no one saw how I worried. How I grieved.

I stood up and paced behind my desk. Sunlight beat in through the window and sweat ran down my back. I rubbed my palm on my chest and leaned over, trying to catch my breath.

"You good?"

"Oh, now you care?" I stood tall again and looked my brother in the eye. Without waiting for his response, I continued. "Like I said, I don't know what I'm doing. I rented a house there, to be near her and her daughter. I leased a car. I mentioned a ring, but then she got sick. I'm not equipped for this, Adam. I'm the good-time guy. I panicked."

Adam stepped close and laid a hand on my back. "Cal, I don't know what I'm doing either, but I can't imagine it's much different than the way Mom loved us. Unconditionally."

This made me laugh. "Maybe you, not me. When I told her I was having a baby boy, she asked if he was going to have a *bris*. Seriously, Ad. Her first question was is he going to have his dick chopped in some covenant with God during a Jewish custom. She knows Shell. She knows she's mixed race. She knows she's not Jewish. That was another way of saying she didn't approve."

I started pacing.

"Sit down," Adam said. He sat across from me and stared me in the eye. "It's a lot for her. I married a non-Jew, and I'm having a baby with this woman.

You're having a baby out of wedlock with another non-Jew. The skin color isn't the problem for Mom. It's the religion. She found solace in the temple group, and now she feels like she'll be an outcast."

"That's absurd. She doesn't realize everyone will be happy she's a grandma. My fucking baby isn't even going to live in this country. And you come and go from here."

"We know that. This will take time. When I spoke with Mom, I told her it was Shell's choice how she handled your son's private parts."

"Thanks." I swallowed my pride. This was my brother. He was the caretaker, and I was the fuckup.

Adam shook his head. "I can see what you're thinking, that I take care of everything. That's not the truth. You built this business here. You find our clients, who pay us more money than I ever thought I'd earn. You're a good guy, Cal. Get your head out of your ass. Shell got sick. She needed you to take care of her, not run away. It's time you started thinking about getting old with someone."

"Oh, shut it. You made your point. Now, can we go to lunch so we can send our brood to college without worries?"

He gave me a quick nod and stood.

"So, a girl?" I asked him on our way out of the office.

"A girl. Rylan seemed disappointed, said she would mess a daughter up, but after some talking, she's set on the idea."

It was my turn to nod and smile.

What the fuck did I know? Apparently, nothing.

Later that night, I called Shell and said hi. It wasn't like we hadn't been talking the last week and a half, but our conversations had been strained. Once again, it was my responsibility to clear the air and apologize.

After we said our hellos and how-are-yous, I recapped the conversation with Adam, saying that I wanted to be more transparent, and mentioned that I was a shitty person to deal with.

"I'm not selfish. I just don't always get it," I had to admit.

Shell sighed. "I know. It hurt, though. This is why I didn't want to do this. I'm getting attached and, well, I don't know where your head is at."

Sitting on my rooftop balcony—because I lived in a primo bachelor pad in the Meatpacking District—I started to say where my head was at.

"Well, I'll tell you," was all I got out before I heard a deep voice in the background.

"All done," he seemed to say.

Then Shell said, "One sec," and I heard some murmuring.

*What the fuck?*

All of a sudden, I was pacing and sweating for the second time today.

The lights of New York sparkled below me, irritating me further. The world was going on down there while mine might be falling apart up here, all because I was an idiot.

My thoughts raged and roared in my head while I waited for Shell to get back to me.

"Cal?" She returned to the call and said my name with a question at the end as if this were my fault, but I wasn't the one keeping her waiting.

My temper flared. Knowing it wouldn't serve me in this scenario, I channeled what I thought Adam would do, and said evenly, "I'm here."

"Sorry. I'm sure that came across poorly."

"Is everything okay?"

"Yes. Everything is fine. You were saying something?"

*That's how she's going to handle this?*

Looking up at the night sky, I collected myself.

"Shell, I was going to ask you to come visit. With Weezie," I quickly added. "That was where my head was at. I wanted to fly you here. Private, if necessary. But now my head is in a different place. Like, why is there a strange man in your house? At night? With Weezie there? And why did you cover the phone to speak with him?"

Yes, I'd messed up a thousand times already, but Shell was mine. *Isn't she?*

She cleared her throat. "My sink was leaking all over the floor. It didn't start until after five. I tried to turn the water off, but I couldn't get the right angle to reach the knob without hurting my belly. Weezie wanted to call my dad, but I didn't want to upset him."

"So, why didn't you call me?"

She laughed. "Caleb, you're in America. I'm here. What were you going to do?"

"Simple. I would have called Jack."

"Jack can't rush over here on a whim. He's not an errand boy and he has a life. So, I called Tony."

*I knew it.*

"I'm sure he rushed right over."

"It's not like that. He knows I don't care for him in that way. He's a friend. That's all."

"Oh, I'm sure he knows."

"All he did was replace the pipe."

I felt my palms clench. "And Weezie, watching men come in and out of the house?" I could feel the pulse pounding in my neck. *Thump-thump. Thump-thump.*

"She was getting ready for bed. She felt bad about that because she'd been helping me use a bucket to catch the water."

"I get that I'm not there, but it's my job to take care of you and Weezie. Mine," I said, although I had zero authority to do so.

"No, Cal, it's not your job. I'm not yours, and neither is Weez."

"Listen, stop. Please. I'm sorry I messed up, and I'm sure that's why you didn't call me. But I want to know these things. You could have stayed at my house. In fact, you should."

"*Grrr.*" She actually growled into the phone, and if I had to be honest, I'd admit it hit me everywhere. Pained my heart and made my dick hard. I loved— no, admired—this woman's conviction. Love wasn't a word I was equipped to use.

Shell scoffed. "We can't pick up and move into your mansion. We live here."

"Listen, I'm going to make things right." Yes, I ignored her comments on living in my mansion. It was going to happen.

"We'd like to come," she said next, taking control of the conversation.

"Come?"

"To see you."

I went from wanting to punch someone to pounding my free fist into my chest. "Great."

I'd deal with Tony's faux friendship another time.

"What about July Fourth week?"

"That's a week from now."

"So? I'll arrange it. Weezie will love it."

"Okay."

I wasn't sure how the conversation had turned so quickly, but I liked where it was heading.

"Are you sure you want Weezie to come?" Shell asked warily. "She can be a lot. She'll make a mess of your place. If we're going to stay there, I mean. I guess that's presumptuous."

"Shell." Her name came out as a mewl. This woman could be frustrating.

"Okay, okay," she said again.

"You're staying with me. We can handle the sleeping arrangements however you want. Of course, I want time alone with you, but I get the whole picture. It may seem like I'm slow on the uptake, and sometimes I am, but Weezie is part of the package. A great part," I added. "I get that being with you includes Weezie, and I'm cool with that too. It's summer. We can take a beach day, and maybe go to the Statue of Liberty." I was rambling, pulling a bunch of touristy things out of my ass.

"Oh yes, she'd like that."

"Good. It's settled then."

"Cal?" Shell's voice was full of apprehension, and I wished she didn't feel that way with me—ever.

"Yes? Ask anything you want, Shell."

"Are there nanny services? I assume so. Maybe we can have a date night? I mean, I've never used a service like that, but I assume they're vetted."

"Yes, there are. I know because of clients. Good ones. Excellent ones. Date night, it is. Let me look into flights, and we can talk more about this tomorrow."

"You mean, your assistant?"

She had me there. "Not this time. I'm going to handle the flights myself. He may handle the rest, but I have to work."

Shell chuckled. "It's fine. I was only kidding."

I absorbed the easiness that had settled over us, relaxing into it.

"Night, Cal," rang in my ear and went straight to my groin.

"Night, Shell. I'll touch base in the morning." Before we hung up, though, an idea came over me. "You know what? Can you hold the phone to your belly?"

"Yes." Her tone was quiet, as if she suspected what I wanted to do, and it touched her. "Here I go."

"Hi there, fella. It's your dad. I can be an idiot, but it doesn't mean I don't love ya."

I didn't wait to say anything more to Shell. This whole scene was too much for me to make sense of, so I hung up.

For the first time in my life, I was acting and living based on feelings.

And it didn't feel bad at all.

# CHAPTER TWENTY-FIVE

• July •

*Shell*

Bright sunlight hit my face as Weezie and I stepped off the small charter jet that had brought us to New York.

I'd texted Cal that we could fly commercial, but he wouldn't hear of it. Instead, Weezie and I flew to the States like rock stars. We were ushered into a small customs area where they checked our passports before leading us through a door where Cal was waiting on the other side.

It was a Friday afternoon, and he'd insisted on meeting us, saying the city was shutting down as everyone escaped to the shore for the weekend.

"Cal!" Weezie ran to him like he was the ice-cream truck. Then again, he was better with private planes and vacations.

"Hey, Weez. Welcome to New York," he said, bending down to give her a hug.

I got a "Hey" when I got close, and then without warning, Cal pulled me in for a kiss. His arm wrapped around me, and his lips pressed to mine. It was the first time we'd been intimate like this in front of Weezie, and when we broke free, she didn't seem the least bit fazed.

Cal leaned close and whispered in my ear, "Welcome to New York," then brushed his lips along my cheek. "Come on."

He took Weezie's hand and led us toward the doors. Outside, he pulled his phone out of his pocket. "I've gotta call for our ride."

I nodded like this was an everyday thing for me, but it wasn't.

"Excited?" he asked Weezie while we waited.

She nodded. "Do you live near the American Girl doll store?"

"Weez! I told you maybe," I said.

I'd warned her not to ask. The dolls were expensive, and he'd already given her so much.

"I love the doll you gave me," she said to Cal, pretending she hadn't heard me, I'm sure. "But they have all kinds. Gymnastics dolls and dolls with pigtails, and they do cool things like skateboard and teach. I really want another one because Sandy has two and we could play with them all together . . ."

Thankfully her rambling was interrupted by a large black SUV rolling up to the curb and a driver getting out to open the door for us. "Mr. Stern. Ms. Light."

He quickly took our luggage, which I only just realized Cal had retrieved for us. I'd been so caught up with the kiss, I would have left without it.

"One sec," Cal told Weezie. "In the car, we'll finish."

Which was exactly what we did. After another five minutes of detail on the dolls and that there was a store and a restaurant, Cal was on the phone with his assistant, who I learned was named Duncan, and we had a reservation for lunch the next day at American Girl Dolls.

"Would you like some water?" Cal asked me, leaning forward and taking a bottle that had been chilling in the center console.

"Can I have a sip?" Weezie hollered from the third row where a booster seat had been installed for her.

As we whizzed along busy streets and then through a tunnel into the city, I took in the sights. Looking back at Cal, I asked, "You drive in the Caymans, but not here?"

"No, I use this car service. We have a contract. I don't even keep a car, but after visiting you, I think it would be nice to have one to get away with around here . . . get a chance to breathe fresh air."

I nodded again as if this was part of my normal life.

Weezie piped up. "Cal, do you have an elevator?"

"I do," he said to my daughter, who was fascinated with city life. "I live at the top of my building. It used to be a factory with offices above. Now it's where people live."

"Do you have Coke?"

*Oh, Weezie.*

"Sure do."

"Duncan?" I asked, thinking Cal didn't grocery shop.

"No, Amber, my housekeeper stocked us up. I gave her the long weekend off, but you may meet her next week. She's been with me for three years. Tired?" Cal asked me, mistaking my quiet for sleepiness rather than being overwhelmed.

"No, I feel good."

"Hungry? We can stop for a late breakfast."

"Yes!"

I didn't have a chance to get in a word after that because Weezie was asking for pancakes.

Cal asked the driver to take us to somewhere called Sarabeth's.

After he wowed us there with pancakes and eggs and chocolate milk, we went to Cal's place, which was the biggest apartment I'd ever seen with views I'd never imagined. Weezie rode the elevator up and down for ten minutes before settling on a chair on his private rooftop deck with a glass bottle of Coke.

"She's asleep," I told Cal, who was sitting on the couch nursing a Scotch.

"She was comfortable?"

Sitting at the other side of the sofa, I nodded. "She said her bed was the biggest, fluffiest thing she's ever seen."

Weezie was staying in the guest room in a queen-size bed complete with a fluffy off-white duvet and about a thousand throw pillows. I wouldn't even let her take a cup of water in there.

"I could have made it a little more girly."

"Stop, Cal. She's happy. Today was probably the best day of her life."

He set his drink down and moved closer. "And you? Did you have a good day?" He slid his palm down my cheek and brought his lips to mine.

The kiss was slow, gentle, tender, yet full of unspoken promise. Now that my stomach was under better control, my hormones were back in full swing and ready for what he was silently promising. I nodded while he kept kissing me.

When he broke free, he said, "Good. I'm glad you're here. I've never really shared this space."

"It's beautiful. Or handsome, I should say."

"I didn't decorate it."

This made me giggle. "I didn't think so."

I wanted to ask if Sophia had spent much time here, but why? I was here now with Weezie and carrying his baby.

Continuing to cradle my cheek in his palm, he asked, "Was Weezie okay with your sleeping arrangements? Did you mention anything?"

This man was such an enigma. I imagined he was a powerful force when it came to his career, and I knew him to be a lover of life. A party boy when time allowed, yet he could be incredibly passionate when it wasn't called to his attention. I didn't even think he knew he did it.

I took a deep breath, and his free palm slid over my belly, presumably massaging our child.

"I'm a little worried because she's so *go with the flow* when it comes to this, but Weezie is usually all about routine. Maybe it's because Ricky just up and disappeared, and she's searching for a replacement. I don't know. I'm not an expert, for sure."

"Shell, you're perfect, a great mom," he whispered to me.

"I don't know about that, but I said I would be staying down the hall in your room, and she said *I know*. No questions, no rambling, nothing. All very unlike Weez."

"Maybe she senses you're happy, and that makes her happy."

"Maybe."

"I don't want to pressure you. I can stay here, on the couch."

"Caleb." His full name tasted like honey coming from my mouth. "Don't be absurd. I'm here. I've been missing you."

"And I've been missing you," he said before kissing me again.

He tasted like mint and Scotch. We'd had Japanese takeout at his counter for dinner—sushi for him, udon noodles for me, and fried rice for Weezie. I'd watched him pop a peppermint in his mouth when we were done and wished it was my tongue. Now it was.

Our mouths danced along each other as my heartbeat sped up. Outside his window, the sky was darkening with dusk. Inside, the lights were dimmed and soft music came from the TV—it was a setting I never saw myself in, but I was here.

"I want you so fucking bad," he murmured into my lips.

"I want you back."

For a moment longer, we kissed and groped like two high school kids who hadn't seen each other in a long while.

"Let's go to my room, yeah? For some privacy," he said.

I nodded, and the next thing I knew, I was being swooped up in his arms. "Cal, I'm too heavy."

"Shhh."

He made his way to his room, me safe in his hold. Once inside, he gently laid me on the bed.

"One sec," he whispered and went to shut the door. "This okay?"

"Yes, please come here." I wasn't one to beg, but it had been a while.

He lay down next to me, running his hand under my shirt and over my belly, stopping for a beat before traveling south, then smoothing over my bra. "Sex is okay. I read it in my books."

"It's more than okay," I said, my voice husky with want. When he lifted my white T-shirt over my head and took in my plain bra, I explained. "It's pretty much the only one that fits right now."

"Perfection."

His mouth came down to meet my nipple, first over the bra, and then he slid the cup down to reveal my skin. He blew a warm breath over it, causing a chill to settle over me. Then his mouth came down on my nipple again, twirling, laving . . . whatever it was, it was decadent. He was careful not to climb on top of me, staying close to my side.

His name came out on a breath from me, and he looked up.

"Take your shirt off," I said softly. "I want to touch you."

He obliged, paying attention to my other nipple while my hands grazed his back. Then he slid down next to me, dragging my maternity capris with him, revealing a turquoise lace thong. At least I'd put on sexy panties.

A growl erupted from Cal's chest as he took me in, and then in a flash, he ripped them off of me. "Sorry, I'll buy you more," he said before running his tongue along my inner thigh.

I didn't know when I'd ended up in a romance novel. Panty-ripping wasn't something that happened to me, but I liked it.

I didn't have time to dwell on it, because Cal found my core with his tongue and his finger slid inside me at the same time. My head fell back, and I could feel myself coming undone within moments. I tried to hold back, wanting to savor this.

"Shell, give it to me," Cal whispered. Explaining how he knew, he said, "I can feel you starting to quiver, and then you clench up. Let go for me."

He swiped over my hottest area, and I went off like a rocket. Turning my head to the side, I moaned into the pillow. I didn't know how soundproof these walls were, but I didn't want to wake Weezie.

Cold air rushed over me as Cal stood and dropped his pants to the floor, his belt buckle clanking against the hardwood. Next, he shrugged off his boxer briefs and was naked except for the bulky Rolex on his wrist.

He knelt at my feet and ran his tongue around my ankle—the one where I wore the shell anklet he gave me. Kissing his way up my calf, he spent time around my knee, coming back over my body, spending a beat or ten, reminding me what he just did to my core, and my desire began to ramp up again. He slid back up next to me and gathered me in his arms, pulling me over him, seating me above his groin.

Like a pair who did this all the time, I raised slightly on my knees and he positioned himself. I didn't waste time sliding onto his length. I needed to rush. A fire was raging inside me, and the only way to put it out was to douse myself in Cal.

I rode him quickly, bracing myself on his chest, his hands coming up to cup my breasts.

"Slow down, babe," he said, taking my hip in his hand and stilling me.

He reached up and brought my head down to meet his, where we kissed with my belly between us. He used his hand on my hip to guide me to a languid pace, lifting his hips to create friction.

We moved like that a while until I couldn't take it, and sat up to pick up speed on my own. Cal's head finally fell back, showing me all the veins in his neck as he climaxed.

I felt myself go off right as he began, which wasn't the norm for me, but I was so turned on and my feelings were way too deep when it came to this man.

I'd been trying to control those feelings, but afterward, he took my hand and ushered me to a warm shower. There, he cleaned me off, then wrapped me in a robe and cuddled me, whispering, "You're magnificent. I'm so happy you're here."

At that moment, I knew I couldn't control a damn thing.

# CHAPTER TWENTY-SIX

*Cal*

The three of us were in the back of a chauffeured car on our way to the Hamptons for the day when my phone rang.

As Shell set up a movie for her daughter in her booster seat behind us, I was quietly wondering how I would sleep without Shell in my bed. She and Weezie had been in the city for three days and would be leaving soon, and thinking about it caused a twinge in my chest. She was turned around, helping Weezie in the third row, her gorgeous profile on display.

I looked at the caller ID and sighed. Seeing it was my mom, I debated for a second whether to answer. Deciding that if I didn't, she'd call back, I accepted the call. "Hi, Mom."

Shell's head popped up, her eyes meeting mine. All she knew was my mom was unsettled about my current life circumstances.

"Caleb, you haven't called," my mom said, starting with the guilt.

I'd sent her a pointed email, removing emotion from my words like a well-trained lawyer, stating that the baby Shell and I were expecting was her grandson and she needed to get behind it all. Her nonresponse was her way of backing down. I knew my mom. She'd wait for me to reach out to her and say how much I loved her, forgetting the whole incident ever happened.

"I know. Shell's been here with Weezie, and I've been showing them the city."

This was when the sweat would normally pour down my back, when nerves would slam me over the thought of my life changing. But nothing happened. In fact, my unease settled, and I felt a calmness wash over me.

"I know," Mom said. "Adam called and said he heard you were having fun."

Now I saw why she called. She knew I'd have an audience and wouldn't be able to speak my mind.

Mom continued. "He and Rylan are going to Lake Michigan for the Fourth and invited me, but I have a cookout with the temple."

Adam and Rylan had called the day before to say hi and to let us know they were heading back to Grand Cayman for August and September. Rylan wanted to set up some projects at work before their baby girl arrived around Christmas.

"We're on our way to the Hamptons. I figured the girls should see an American beach," I said into the phone.

Over the last few days, I'd started calling Shell and Weezie *the girls*, and it made Weezie giggle every time. Right now, she wore Beats headphones over her ears, her hair smoothed back in a braid, her eyes focused on a Disney movie. It was part of the setup with the car company, and a very smart idea. We had two hours to drive.

"Oh, that's nice," Mom said. "How does she feel?"

My brows popped up. It was the first time my mom had inquired.

"She's feeling well. Stomach is all settled, but we're skipping the boat adventure today."

Mom rattled off a bunch of questions about whether Shell was showing, was she excited to have a boy, and avoided asking any religion-related questions.

Shell watched me intently but didn't interrupt. Whether she said it or not, she'd been uneasy about my mom's opinion of her.

"She's showing," I said, thinking it may get me in trouble. "She's more than halfway, so of course she is, but she looks beautiful."

Just then Weezie tossed off her headphones, "Mom, look! Lilo lives with her sister and Stitch is kind of like a little brother. Like me."

"Is that Weezie?" Mom asked, not missing a beat.

"Of course. She's telling us something about a movie."

For a moment, I couldn't believe this was me having this conversation. A few years ago, I rented a bungalow in the Hamptons for the Fourth and had a big party, nothing but bikinis and booze.

"Let me say hello. She's going to be the baby's sister. I met her at Adam's wedding."

Regret filled me over picking up the call.

Clearing my throat, I turned toward Shell. The sunlight filtered through the window beside her, making her skin shine and her cheeks glow. She'd also pulled her hair back in a braid and was wearing an orange sundress. One thing I was learning was how to temper my desire to get Shell naked with Weezie around.

"My mom wants to say hi to Weez," I said.

Still with her headphones off, Weezie perked up. "Me? Yay! I met your mom when I was the flower girl. She has shiny blond hair like Elsa."

I nodded, then mouthed to Shell, *Is that okay?*

She nodded.

"Put it on FaceTime," my mom demanded, bossy as usual.

"Really?"

"Yes, Caleb."

I turned the phone to face me and tapped the icon for FaceTime.

I waited for my mom to respond and saw she was sitting on her patio, her hair pristine, and I'm sure a perfect outfit on. My mother was a perfectionist. I wasn't sure how she'd raised triplets as a single mom, but she had. Remembering that gave me faith in my own ability to parent.

I handed the phone to Shell as my mom spoke.

"Hi, Weezie. Remember me? I'm going to be your baby brother's grandma, and so I'll sort of be yours too."

Weezie took the phone from Shell and smiled at the screen. "I remember. Do you remember me? I wore the pretty dress at Ry's wedding."

"I do. Are you enjoying New York?"

"I got another American Girl doll."

This made Shell immediately roll her eyes and me laugh. The new doll was the highlight of Weezie's trip, and a bone of contention with Shell. She'd said I was spoiling her daughter, buying her another doll, and I'd thrown my hands up in the air and said, "What else am I supposed to do?"

"Her name is Maritza. She looks a little like me, but I wasn't allowed to bring her to the beach today. She would get dirty, and Mom said I have to keep her clean."

My mom listened and then said, "I'll have to meet her sometime. My daughter, Becca, loved dolls. She used to cut all their hair, though. They'd be bald by the time she was done."

"Shit," I murmured. We hadn't spoken about my deceased sister to Weezie. Weezie giggled but looked confused, so I reached back and took the phone. "Okay, Mom. We'll talk soon."

"Wait," she said quickly. "Let me say something to Shell."

I knew she'd get her way, so I gave Shell the phone.

"Shell, do you like New York? If so, come back and tie this guy up. I need you and your daughter in my life. I didn't realize how much I missed having a little girl around."

Shell glanced at me, her cheeks darkening. "Uh, I like New York, but I'm not tying anyone up."

I didn't know if she really meant that or was saying it for effect, but she certainly had tied me up.

Taking the phone and the control again before this became a disaster, I said, "Mom, we'll tie everything up later. Happy Fourth," I said and disconnected.

*Sorry*, I mouthed to Shell.

Of course Weezie asked, "Who is Becca?"

I didn't even try to explain. This sort of thing was way out of my skillset.

Shell spent some time explaining how I had a sister in heaven, and how much I loved her. Weezie asked why she was in heaven, and Shell said simply it was a rare thing that happened sometimes, but not to worry because it wasn't going to happen to anyone she knew.

When they were done, Weezie happily went back to her movie.

I grinned at Shell. "You're amazing."

My mom was right. It was time to get tied down. I was going to ask Shell to marry me.

That night, as we all lounged on a blanket on the beach, staring up at the stars and the fireworks booming, Weezie sticky from ice cream and Shell snuggled up between my legs, I kissed her neck from behind.

"Hey, Shell," I whispered.

"Yeah?"

"I love you." I'd never said it before. Never thought I'd feel it, but I did. "And your daughter. And our son."

She half turned, the moonlight reflecting off the earrings I'd bought for her. "I love you too."

We stayed like that a while, me holding Shell close and Weezie next to us. No bikinis or booze, but perfect.

Later, Weezie fell asleep on the car ride back. I kicked myself for not renting a house in the Hamptons, but the girls seemed happy being chauffeured back to the city. We had plans to make pancakes the next morning and then go to the Central Park Zoo. It would be our last day together.

When we got home, I carried Weezie to bed before Shell dressed her in her pajamas and slipped her under the covers. The little mogwai smelled like sunscreen, sand, and bubblegum ice cream—a day well done. I couldn't help but be captivated watching Shell kiss her daughter's forehead, mumbling sweet nothings before slipping out of the room.

Afterward, I undressed Shell and helped her into a warm shower, then joined her, taking my time soaping her body. As I caressed her stomach, something moved. I jolted, which of course sent Shell into a fit of laughter.

"That's your little animal in there. He likes to move around when there's water running. He's a beach baby."

"Can I?" I asked, my hand hovering over her abdomen, and she nodded.

I placed my hand carefully on her belly and moved it around. Sure enough, the little guy gave me another jab.

My lips immediately sought Shell's. I couldn't find words to describe how I was feeling, so I showed her with my mouth and my tongue. Later, I made love slowly to her under the blankets.

We fell asleep naked and tangled in each other's arms, which sure was a shock when Weezie came wandering into our room the next morning.

Of course, I nearly fell out of bed, but Shell handled it like a champ, sending Weezie to go get her a glass of water, then she quickly jumped up and tossed on a robe.

Everything was so perfect. I hated that the end of our little vacation was approaching.

# CHAPTER TWENTY-SEVEN

*Shell*

"**M**om, *is C*al going to be here when I'm done at art camp?"

"Yes, baby girl."

I took a swig of my decaf iced tea and pressed the cool glass to my forehead. The heat, my nerves, the extra weight, all of it was getting the best of me.

"Are we going swimming at his house? Please! Please!" Weezie danced around on one foot and then the other while pleading.

"I'm sure if you would like to swim, we can," I said, but I also needed a dip in the pool myself. August heat had fallen on the island, and being pregnant was losing its allure super quick.

"Yes!" She fist-pumped the air, which made me wonder *if she'd turned into a prete*en overnight.

Weezie had been Cal's number one fan since the New York trip. She cried when we said good-bye, clinging to him at the airport. Cal held her tight, acting like he was being strong for her, but I thought he was absorbing all of her affection. It was clear something had shifted during our visit, but it was time to go back to reality. He promised to call every night, and he'd kept true to his word.

Cal told me one night he'd decided to settle in and do a lot of work during July while the city was quieter, so he *could come to the Caymans for an extended stay in* August. We hadn't discussed what his plans were when the b*aby came, nor had we said I love you again since the night on the beach.*

"*Can we stay at Cal's like we did in New York? It's really nice there,*" Weezie *said, pushing for more. She*'d mentioned it before, and I kept saying no. I knew my daughter better than to think she'd give it a rest.

I wasn't sure what exactly was making me hesitant. Staying there felt wrong—almost like a booty call. Then again, wasn't that how this whole damn situation had started?

My phone rang with a text. It was Rylan, who was also back on the island. She planned to *stay here until early October, and then go to the States to have the baby.*

*Do you have any banana syrup?*

*Somehow in between* growing a baby, raising Weezie, traveling to New York, and talking with Cal on the phone, I was also seri*ously growing my s*yrup business. I'd play around with different recipes at the coffee shop, and then the factory would do a test run.

So far, every flavor was selling out as soon as we released it. The manufacturer's direct sales were amazing, and I handled the local sales on the island. With the help of Teddi, I'd set up an Instagram page and shop, and some days I barely had the time to manage it.

I have a case at the coffee shop. Do you need some?

She wrote back right away with ten praying-hands emojis.

Yes! I'm planning this bridal brunch and the bride is allergic to coconut, so we're doing banana chocolate chip pancakes. A touch of that syrup to the batter will make them pop.

Another thing the factory and I noticed was many chefs were using my syrups due to their natural nature to give a little zing to recipes, but I still loved enhancing coffees with them the most. Of course, I was focused on paying Cal back the capital he put up, and he refused to discuss it. Things were going so well, I hoped to have enough to repay them both soon.

I'm heading in now after I drop Weez at the Y. Want to swing by?

Yes, I do. And we can take a picture of our bumps together.

Rylan was straight-up obsessed with her baby bump, but I wasn't. Maybe because my guy was only part-time.

No more bump pics, I texted back, but I knew better.

An hour later, after she promised to speak with Adam about my paying the brothers back, Rylan was standing with her camera held above us, making a boomerang and then posting it on Instagram with the caption *besties*. Of course, she sneaked a bottle of syrup in the photo too, and tagged my brand. Later today, I'd have orders to fill as a result.

We were tucking our shirts down as, "Hey, babe, I'm here," rang through the store.

"Oh no, no, I liked that view," Cal said with a wink.

In seconds, I was yanked into his arms, and he was planting a kiss on me.

Wiggling free from him, I saw Jack was here too. "Oh, Jack, this guy is never going to let you go," I said, then asked him, "Want a coffee?"

Jack nodded, and as I started making him a large, he smiled. "You have the coconut syrup?"

"Of course I do. It's the tourists' favorite too."

"Like your guy here, a tourist," Jack teased.

Cal pretended to snarl. "Hey, I have a car here and a house."

"I don't see you using the car," Jack said, joking back.

"All right, all right," Cal said, and I glanced over to take him in.

He looked delicious. His hair was a bit longer, his skin tanned from being on his rooftop, I assumed. He wore a white polo shirt and khaki shorts, along with his driving loafers. I needed to get him some flip-flops.

I poured Cal a coffee without asking, adding some syrup and half-and-half, and handed it over.

"How's my dude?" he said, motioning to my belly.

"Safe and sound."

"And my little lady?"

"Wants to go swimming later."

"Her wish is my command."

"Don't I know it. You're spoiling her, Cal."

"So? Would you rather I be mean?"

"Stop. You don't have a mean bone in your body."

Rylan and Jack watched our banter, their heads pinging between us.

Jack looked at me. "Okay, folks, do you have city boy, here? Can I take off?"

"I have some work, but I can drop you at your place," I said to Cal.

He nodded and then saluted Jack. "Thanks, man."

"Thanks, babe," Rylan said to me, kissing my cheek.

"Oh, Jack, can you carry this out for Ry?" I motioned toward the case of syrup.

"Is it going to the hotel? I'll take it. Going there now."

"Can you?" Rylan asked. "I need to stop and grab some samples from the linen place."

"No prob."

"Leave it with Tony. I'll text him what to do."

I noticed Cal's fists clench at the mere mention of Tony. The guy was bent out of shape over nothing. Yeah, Tony had tried to date me for a hot minute, but I wasn't into him like that. That didn't mean he wasn't a good guy. He was one of the better ones, and happened to be Rylan's closest friend, so for better or worse, he was part of our lives.

"Will do," Jack said, grabbing the case and was out the door.

Rylan followed behind, calling out, "I'll let Adam know you're here. Dinner tomorrow? Our place?"

Cal nodded, then came close, backing me into the counter, his arms on either side of me. "Finally alone. Tell me, how are you, Shell?"

"I'm good. Told you already."

He pushed an errant hair behind my ear, smoothing his palm over my curly mane. His mouth found my cheek, then my earlobe. "Missed you," he whispered.

I swallowed for fear of what would fall out of my mouth. A whole list of endearments and proclamations ran through my overactive mind.

"Did you miss me?" he asked, his breath hot on my ear.

"Yes," I finally croaked out.

"I don't like this anymore, the separation between us. I thought it would be okay, but it's not."

"Cal—"

"No, don't *Cal* me. I don't like it, but I'm not sure how to fix it. I need to be in New York quite a bit."

"And Weez goes to school," I said, raising a brow.

"I know. I'm working on a solution. Promise you'll think about whatever I dream up?"

His lips hovered close to mine, doing crazy things to my pulse rate. I would have promised anything to secure one more kiss with this man, so I nodded, and he kissed me. We stayed like that for a while, and I was thankful for a lull in the coffee shop until a voice bellowed, interrupting our affections.

Dad spread his arms wide as he came through the front door. "My favorite American is back! Next to your brother, of course," he joked.

"I'm back. Like I said I would be," Cal said.

Cal and my dad shared some kind of moment. I wasn't sure what it was, but I knew better than to ask. Assuming it was about the loan and my urgency to pay everyone back, I kept my thoughts to myself. When it came to these two, I couldn't decide which one was the more stubborn.

"Dad, I'm going to drop Cal at his place and then swing by the Ritz. They have an order to place and want me to take it in person."

"Good, good. You should tell your friends over at the Grand Escape that the Ritz is ordering nonstop," he teased.

"Dad, Rylan was just here. The Grand remains our number one customer on the island."

"I know, baby girl."

My dad smiled, the corners of his eyes crinkling, and I thought how grateful I was for a father who loved me unconditionally.

With this thought came sadness. It struck me in the gut over Weezie's hurt about how Ricky had walked out on her. Cal's spoiling her was sweet and endearing, but it wasn't a replacement for unconditional love. This was why I had to consider her with every decision I made, maybe even more so.

"Wherever you just went in your head, come back to me," Cal said, squeezing my hand.

"Okay. Let's go," I muttered while walking toward the door, then stopped short. "Oh shoot, I have to get my purse. Pregnancy brain."

My dad and Cal exchanged another one of their looks, and I made a mental note to call Dad later.

Once I had my purse, Cal and I headed out. Of course he asked for the keys and started to drive.

"Oh shit, I forgot," he said. "I have to pick up something at the Grand. They're holding something for me there."

We came to the roundabout. He exited toward the resort where I first met him, where Rylan worked, and where she met Adam at the end of her bar. It was where Adam and Rylan were married, and where Cal and I had first discussed my being pregnant. The Grand Escape was at the epicenter of our short history.

We pulled into the drive, and of course Tony was at the valet stand, since he ran the department. I held my breath, waiting to see what would happen next.

Surprising me, Cal quickly jumped out and told me, "Wait here." Only stopping briefly to say something to Tony, he barely came to a stop before entering the hotel.

I took a deep breath, worried Cal had left too much work behind and was having some materials shipped to the hotel. There wasn't a lot of time left to wonder, though, because he wasn't gone long. He hurried back out carrying two packages, a small box and a bigger one.

"This one is for you."

He handed me the little one after he slid in the car, and my heart did a cartwheel. I didn't think it could be a ring, but I wondered if maybe it was.

Waves of emotion crashed over me like the ocean in the distance. It was high tide over my heart.

"Thank you," I said, my voice a bit shaky.

"Open it," he said.

With even shakier hands, I opened the top to find a small pouch. I opened it and tipped out what was inside, surprised to see the most beautiful band I'd ever seen. Seashells crafted out of rose gold ran around the whole band, acting as the base, with different colored stones outlining the ridges of each shell.

"Oh my. It's gorgeous, but . . ." I didn't know what to say.

*What does it mean? What is it? A friendship ring?*

"It's a wedding band. Not an engagement ring," Cal said, taking in my silence.

There we sat in my car, in the valet circle at the Grand, the air-conditioning humming, and the world fading away around us.

"Why?" I asked. I'd lost my words moments earlier, and now my question made zero sense. "I mean, it's gorgeous, and must have taken days to craft. Look how intricate each one of these shells are . . . it's the most special ring I've ever seen."

"Shell, I'm not asking you to marry me right now."

"Oh." Clearly, I wasn't getting what was happening, or I was in the middle of some cruel joke.

"Do you want to know why?" Cal asked, then quickly continued without letting me say a word. "Because you and Weez come together as a package, and she needs to be a part of the decision. You may not say it enough, but I've come to see it, the way you take care to be sure Weezie always feels loved. She deserves all the love."

"Caleb—"

But he still wouldn't let me get a word in, which was annoying and cute.

"Listen, I'm a jerk and can be stupid when it comes to this sort of thing, but the last few weeks without you have been awful. I can't do it. I need you with me. It's a lot to ask, which is why I'm giving you this wedding band first. It's an eternity band, they told me, the way the stones and shells go all the way around, and that's exactly what I have in mind. An eternity with you. This band lets you know that I'm already signed up for all of that."

My head was spinning. I wasn't sure if it was a proposal . . . or a proclamation.

"It's a prequel. A forward to the proposal coming. A moment for the two of us before we have our moment with Weezie."

I stared at him, trying to figure out how he'd read my mind.

"Oh. It's beautiful," I said, looking at the ring. "Your words were more beautiful. They were enough."

"They weren't," he said, shoving his hand through his hair. "You see, I need you to move to New York. Adam's role makes it easier for him to travel around, but I'm the front man, and I need to be in New York. I know it's a lot to ask, Shell, but you could come back and forth as you want, and could work or not work or whatever you wanted there. I want to see my son grow up alongside his sister, and to spend my nights with you. Please, just consider it."

His expression was strained, concerned, as if I wouldn't consider his offer.

Taking a moment, I thought it over. "It's a lot. I admit that. I've never lived anywhere else, and I have this business now, and my parents, and Weezie has friends. But I'll think about it."

My words ran into each other. If you'd told me when Cal and I had our first passionate night together that I'd someday be thinking about moving to the States with him, I would have howled with laughter.

Yet, here we were talking about it.

"One more thing," I said, giving him a serious look. "You can't buy Weezie every American Girl doll in the store."

This broke the tension, making Cal laugh before he leaned over my center console and kissed me. We were like two teens in a parked car, except we weren't in a private location. It wasn't long before a horn dragged us from our stupor.

Cal started the car, and before he drove off, glanced at me with a grin. "Maybe just half the dolls in the store."

I looked out the window, wondering what the heck had just happened.

# CHAPTER TWENTY-EIGHT

Shell dropped me off at the house, and I wanted her to come inside and get naked.

"We have to stop kissing in cars like this," she said, disentangling herself from me. She leaned back in her passenger seat, but made no move to switch to the driver's side.

"We don't have to stop kissing at all. Come in, and we can kiss and more," I said, running my nose along her cheek. The box with the band sat in her lap, under her belly.

When she caught me glancing at it, she said, "I didn't know whether I should put it on or not."

"No pressure. This is up to you. You're charting our course."

"When I don't even know the route," she said, a smile forming on her face.

"You will soon enough. Now, go do your work before I drag you inside and then outside for some skinny-dipping."

Shell snorted out a laugh. "With my belly getting in the way."

"I love that belly, and I love you," I said, which made her mouth drop open. When she gave me a confused look, I asked, "What?"

She shied away from looking at me, her loose hair falling in front of her profile. "We haven't . . . we haven't said it again since we did the first time."

"I'm sorry. I thought it was implied. I'll do better."

"No, I was letting my mind get the best of me. Okay, we have to stop making out in cars," she said, changing the subject. "Get out."

I did as I was told, and as she walked in front of the car, I grabbed my other box from the backseat. "What time are you getting Weezie?"

"Three."

"Good. I'll be at your house a little after two, and maybe we can go get her together."

Shell grinned at me. "I'm not going to turn that down, because my daughter may stab me if she found out."

"Go sell some syrups, babe," I said with a wink, then helped her get in the car and watched her drive away.

I had shit to do after I called Adam and thanked him for setting me straight.

"Cal, watch! Look what I learned." Weezie stood at the side of the pool, hands in the air, Shell eyeing her from a nearby chair.

"I'm watching," I hollered back.

"Woo-hoo," she yelled before cannonballing into the pool.

It had taken some time, but I no longer felt as if I had to jump in after her. She broke the water's surface and swam to the side, then climbed out.

"That was a ten," I told her. "Now grab a towel. I have a Coke for you."

I walked over to where Shell was sitting, carrying a cup of soda with a straw for Weezie, and a glass of lemon-lime water for Shell. After wrapping herself in a beach towel, Weezie plopped down on the chaise.

"Your drink, little lady," I teased her, handing her the cup. "And yours, miss," I said to Shell.

"It's like the Grand here," Weezie said. "Pool, drinks, servers getting you stuff."

Shell frowned at her. "Weez, remember when I was a server? Don't talk like you're better than others. It's not nice."

"Okay, Mom," she said, frowning for a second.

I might not listen to Shell when she said not to buy dolls or sodas, but I knew better than to interfere with life lessons.

With an important question to ask, I sat at the end of Weezie's lounger. The little sweetie immediately pulled her knees up to make room for me, sipping on her Coke, happy as a clam.

Taking a big breath, I hoped Shell would be happy any moment. "What do you say we go to dinner later? We can go to the Grand if you want."

"Yes, please, please!" Weezie exclaimed, never one to turn down a good time.

"I can cook here," Shell said, but I shook my head.

"I kind of want to celebrate."

"What?" both of my girls said in unison.

"Well, I was hoping to ask you and Weezie to marry me today."

I kept my gaze focused on Shell when I said it. She wasn't wearing the shell band, but I wasn't upset. I told her to take her time and figure out what she wanted to do.

"Marry?" Weezie asked.

"Yes, I'd very much like to be your stepdad and your mom's husband. Would you like that?"

I knew Weezie still thought about her dad and didn't quite understand why he left, and I didn't want to overstep my boundaries.

"Yes!" She set her Coke down on the table next to her and started dancing around the pool area.

Turning my attention back to Shell, who was still sitting calmly across from me, I stood and then knelt in front of her, snatching Weezie's towel and putting it under my knee on the concrete. With a hand extended, holding the second ring I'd hidden in the larger box to throw Shell off, I spoke with conviction.

"Shell, my darling, will you marry me? Will you allow me to spend the rest of my life adoring you?"

With a smile, she asked, "Did your mom make you do all this?"

I let out a laugh. "No fucking way."

"Language."

I glanced at Weezie dancing around. "I don't think she noticed. And no, my mom didn't make me do a thing. She was happy to hear I was getting around to it."

"And the religion thing?" Shell asked.

"She's happy that I'm happy," I said, and I truly thought my mom was. "She's a survivor, and she's all about growing her family. So, yeah, she's fine."

Shell nodded, a tear slipping from her eye.

"What do you say?" I asked her. "I want to kiss you already. I'm old and still on one knee."

"Mom! Can we live here?" Weezie blurted, interrupting. "With the pool?"

Shell gave me a coy look. "When should I tell her we're moving to New York?"

"Is that a yes?"

After another nod from Shell, I stood and whisked her from the chair as quickly as you can whisk a pregnant woman, and was kissing her when a loud banging came from the front of the house.

"SHELL! Shell! Where the fuck are you?"

When my fiancée's name and those harsh words were shouted from the front yard, I shoved the ring in my pocket, slipping into some instinctive protective mode, and quickly shielded Shell as I growled for Weezie to come to us. She looked a little hurt and confused by my change in demeanor, but her safety was my first concern.

"Weezie, come over to Mommy," Shell said in a strained voice when Weezie hesitated, and she went straight next to her mom and threw her arms around her waist.

"Shell!"

I looked toward her as her name was shouted, and she mouthed, *Ricky*.

"Go in the house," I said, but it was too late.

Her ex came barreling through the gate into the backyard, wielding a baseball bat. He started smashing the fence and whatever else was in his path as he made his way toward us, clipping an umbrella that luckily fell away from us rather than toward us.

"Go in the house," I told my girls through clenched teeth.

"We can't. He'll just follow and trash everything in there too," Shell said.

"What ya doing, lawyer boy? You want to fight me?" Ricky called out, tossing the bat on the ground and holding his fists in the air.

I didn't want to fight him. I might work out and was strong, but I was used to fighting with my words, not my hands. Yet, there was no way I going to look like some kind of pansy in front of Shell.

"You think you can take my family away from me?" he shouted to Shell. "I came back last night, thinking it's time we make up, and found out you're shacking up with this rich guy."

"We're getting divorced, Ricky," she said, but he ignored her.

To Weezie, he said, "Hey, baby, come here and see Daddy."

She shook her head and tightened her grasp on Shell.

"What? You turn my baby girl into a snob, Shelly? I came around last night and went looking for you over at Camila's. Whole place is buzzing. You and Weezie are so happy. You met a fancy fucking lawyer from New York. Having 'nother baby . . . rolling in dough and jewelry. He make you feel all good, Shelly?"

As he moved closer, the stench of alcohol rolled off him.

"That's close enough," I said in a calm tone, knowing yelling would only toss gasoline onto the raging fire in front of us. "You're on private property, and I'm going to have to ask you to leave. I'm only going to ask nicely once."

Ricky scoffed. "Huh-uh. Nope. I want my wife and kid, and if you want to keep them, you're gonna have to pay me good. I need some of life's finer shit too."

"Mommy, I have to go to the bathroom," Weezie said.

Peeking to the side, I saw her hopping on one foot.

"Take her," I said, hoping Shell had enough sense to call the authorities while inside. I added, "It's her legal right," to Ricky, leaving a little bread crumb for Shell.

When they scurried off, I glared at this deadbeat of a man. "You have five seconds to leave here and never contact Shell again. Five . . . four . . . three . . ."

Instead of leaving, though, he said, "I don't think we met. My name's Ricky, the first guy to fuck and knock up Shelly."

I hated the nickname he had for Shell. She was way more fascinating and sophisticated than the way he made her sound.

"Nice to meet you, Ricky. I'm Cal, and like I said, you need to get off my property. You also walked away from Shell and your daughter, so I'm pretty sure you're nobody to them."

"Who are you, Mister High and Mighty?" He picked up the bat again and pounded a nearby lounge chair with it, trying to intimidate me. "All your money and this big fancy house don't mean shit. You got yourself some damaged goods in those two."

I prayed to every god above that Shell was keeping Weezie inside. It would break her heart to hear this.

"Damaged goods, ya hear me?" Ricky lifted the bat in the air and started walking toward me, just as a siren drew closer. A moment later, two men dressed in white uniforms hurried into the yard.

"West Bay Police," one of them called out. "Sir, please put down the weapon."

But Ricky didn't. Instead, he turned and tried to throw it at them, but the bat flew in the air above his own head. I wished it would fall and hit the asshole and knock him unconscious.

Sadly, it didn't, but lucky for Ricky, he was too drunk to defend himself and didn't last long before being wrestled to the ground. Once he was cuffed, the officer yanked him up and held on tight to him.

"Did this man hurt you?" the officer asked me.

"Only the property," I said. "But there's a very frightened little girl inside, along with her terrified pregnant mom."

"Let me get him out of here, and then I'm going to have to ask you to come down to the station and make a statement. Are you pressing charges?"

I nodded. "This is a rental, so in compliance with my agreement, I'm going to have to." I didn't know what Shell would think of that, but I wasn't in the business of protecting Ricky or messing with my welcome in the Caymans.

Shell slipped out of the door without Weezie as they grabbed Ricky and started to guide him toward the police car. One of the officers picked up the bat and put it in a plastic bag, taking it with them for evidence.

Shell rushed over to me. "I'm so sorry."

"Don't be."

"No, I can't subject you to this. My mistakes are not your problems."

"Shell, your ex just harassed you and your daughter, and you're worried about me? Cut it out."

"No, I have to go. I'm taking Weezie home. She's a mess. Her father just showed back up out of nowhere and did that. She thinks you'll hate her for it . . . she's very confused."

Terrified of losing them, I shook my head. "I don't know much about kids, but rushing her out of here is only going to be more confusing."

Tears slid from Shell's eyes, and her hands shook as she looked at the chaise where we'd sat. Her bag sat there open, holding the wedding band box I'd given her earlier. I followed her gaze ghost over it, then watched her grab it and hand it to me.

"All of that, it was beautiful." She motioned to the pool area where I'd proposed. "But it's tainted now, and the rest of my life will be like that because of stupid choices I made. I was a fool to think there was a pot of gold at the end of my rainbow."

She stood on tiptoe and kissed my cheek. It was chaste and quick, friendly, probably signifying an end to a chapter in her mind. She wasn't herself, not thinking straight if she thought I was going to let her go.

"This is ridiculous," I told her. "We're having a baby. I want to marry you. I need to be with you. You're my pot of gold and I'm yours . . . I don't give a shit about him." The arguments rushed from my mouth like water from a hydrant in the middle of the city.

"You will care, eventually. You have a career and a life. Now, I have to go. Seriously." Giving me a sad look, she turned and walked back toward the house, saying, "Go make a statement. You need to."

Weezie ran out of the house, a mess. The little girl gave me a hug while crying her eyes out, breaking my heart. My shirt was soaked with her tears by the time she left with her mom.

The poor girl was as speechless as me. But I was an adult, a grown man who was supposed to be in control. I needed to get my shit together and take charge.

This wasn't how I'd planned the proposal to go, and I didn't like it when things didn't go as planned.

# CHAPTER TWENTY-NINE

*Shell*

Teddi brought me a cup of ginger tea. "Here."

My stomach was upset, nerves flying around inside it like butterflies. While I knew it wasn't good for the baby, my anxiety had a different idea. For the past week, fear had drilled deep into every bone in my body.

"Thank you," I told her. "It was nice of you to come by. Weezie thinks you're so cool, and she's not been herself. For the first time, I don't know what to do."

"Maybe you're doing the wrong thing," Teddi said. "Maybe that's why you're such a mess and at a loss."

I shook my head. Being away from us was what Cal needed. We'd only bring trouble to his life.

Teddi sat down at my feet and lifted them on her lap. "Weezie is upset because she misses Cal. She doesn't understand what happened. She thought she was moving into that rental house with the pool. She's a kid, and Cal was kind to her. He was fun and spoiled her. She never had any of that with Ricky."

Shaking my head again, I muttered, "You sound like Rylan. She's been calling around the clock and making up excuses about why she needs syrup. Then she adds how I'm not thinking clearly, and Weezie loves Cal, and Cal loves us, blah, blah, blah."

Teddi gave me an understanding look. "Shell, my parents are divorced. My dad is an asshole, a grade A asshole. He's a proud member of the girlfriend-of-the-month club, even while he was married. My mom stayed for a while because she thought it was better for me, but it wasn't. Eventually, she met Fred after she and my dad separated. Fred is such a nice guy. He's sweet and generous with his time and affection. I loved Fred growing up, and he didn't even have a pool. He'd help me with homework and answer all my questions without hesitation. My mom couldn't have any more kids, but Fred took me on like his own, and I never looked back."

"Did your dad show up drunk swinging a baseball bat, threatening everyone's safety?" I took a swig of my tea as my stomach rolled.

"No, but being embarrassed and ashamed was part of living with my dad. It's why I came here. To be happy. Of course, I love my mom, Fred, and my grandma, but not my dad. Please stop beating yourself up," she said, running her hand over my foot.

I knew Cal was still on the island. He had a train of people running through here to check on me, including Jack, who offered to pick up groceries. My dad was upset with me for not telling Ricky to shove it and planting a big kiss on Cal right afterward for protecting us. Weezie told my mom we were gonna get married until her dad ruined it all.

I huffed out a frustrated breath. "I can't subject Cal to that guy. What if he does something to hurt Cal's career?"

Teddi frowned at me. "Cal is smart. He won't let that happen. Remember, he deals with jerks for a living. Rich ones. I'm sure he can handle Ricky."

"Ted, I'm meant to be alone."

"You're not, and Weezie definitely isn't. She's in her room thinking she did something wrong. Get your head out of your ass and sort this out, or I'll send Tony over. And when Cal gets a whiff of that, he'll be over here faster than Rylan can run a mile."

My eyes got huge. "No, no. Please don't. I'll deal with this, I promise. Go back to whatever cheery place you came from," I told her, and I meant it.

After she left, I decided I was going to get up and deal with this . . . after a short nap.

Teddi had left Weezie busy coloring upstairs, and that meant I had fifteen minutes to close my eyes. By the time I rested, there would be a new masterpiece for me to hang on the fridge.

When I woke up a short time later, feeling groggy and disoriented, I grabbed my phone. I'd slept much longer than I anticipated, and I shouted for Weezie, terrified she wasn't here.

She came running in from the front porch. "Mom, I'm right here."

"What were you doing out there by yourself? You're not allowed to go outside without telling me."

She had the nerve to stick her hand on her hip and jut it out, staring me down. Just like I would. "I wasn't alone."

"I was here," Cal said, walking through the door.

"Caleb." His name came out like my mouth, dry and fuzzy. "Why?"

He walked toward me and sat where Teddi had been sitting earlier.

"I'm going to play with my American Girl dolls." My daughter ran off before I could grill her any more, leaving behind a small jab.

"I'm supposed to say I just showed up," he said, "but she called me."

"Who? Teddi?"

He shook his head.

"I don't know what you mean. I'm sorry, I must've slept harder than I expected."

"You need rest. You're doing too much. Taking on too much worry."

Cal smoothed his hand down my leg, and I wasn't going to lie, it felt amazing. Chills ran up my spine, and my heart rate spiked at feeling something familiar and good.

"I'm fine," I told him. "I need to work. I quit the restaurant, so I have to do my stuff. My dad spoke to a lawyer about Ricky, and they're working on finalizing the divorce and having him sign away his rights. Once that's done, I'll be less worried."

I closed my eyes and let the emotions take over for a moment.

"I know," Cal said, causing me to sit up and stare. "I'm that lawyer, Shell.

Well, not on record. I'm working with someone here, but you can't be surprised that your dad called me."

My temper flared. "What? And who called you today? Is everyone conspiring against me? No one will let me be."

He stood and walked toward the kitchen. I had no idea what he was doing, but I closed my eyes again.

"Here." Cal was back with a glass of iced tea. "Have a drink."

His tone was so demanding, I sat up and did as I was told.

He took my glass and set it next to me on the end table and then sat down beside me. Laying a hand on my belly, he ran his palm in circles. "Hey, baby, how ya holding up?" he said softly, his voice tender.

"Cal, not now. Don't talk to the baby now. Talk to me. Why can't everyone let this go?"

"Your dad called me on Monday after everything happened. As you know, Ricky spent Friday night in jail. He got out Saturday and went to see your dad."

"Dad didn't tell me."

"Of course not. Your dad isn't in the business of stressing you out. He told Ricky to get the hell out of your life. Ricky said a few choice words back and slunk away."

I shook my head, feeling like I was in a fog. "My parents spent Sunday with me and never mentioned it."

"I know that too. Your dad called on Monday to say he wanted that guy out of his granddaughter's life. For good. So, I met with both of your parents, and then went with them to see a local lawyer. Then they came to you to discuss it, leaving me out of it."

"Oh."

"For the record, I don't accept us being over."

Unable to think of what to say, I simply said, "Oh," again.

Cal ran his lips along my cheek, and I could feel fresh tears sliding down my face.

"Shhh. This mess is going to be done soon. We're not over, you hear me? What we have is too big to ever be over."

Ignoring him, I wallowed a little more in my bad attitude. "I still don't understand how you're here today. I said I didn't want to see you. I can't do this. Us. It's not meant to be. Even though I love you, it's not."

"Your daughter doesn't agree with that. You see, she came downstairs and found you sleeping, so she called me."

I felt my blood pressure climbing. "On what phone?"

"Shell, calm down. Your phone. She knew the passcode, she said, in case of emergency. She felt like this was an emergency because you were so tired and sleeping and needed me. And it was. You do need me, and I need you, and we're doing this. End of discussion."

My throat tightened, and I reached for the tea. Of course, Cal was there to get it for me. After a sip, I could finally talk.

"I can't stand the idea of anything happening to you because of me, Cal. It would destroy me."

"I can't stand the thought of anything happening to you or Weezie because of that fucker, pardon the language, and neither can your dad. We're taking care of you two, protecting you both. Nothing is going to happen to me. I'm a grown man with resources and brains."

"I'm scared," I said softly, staring at my teacup.

"Don't be."

I wasn't sure how he did it, turning every downturn into an upswing, but he did.

"I can't help it, Cal."

His hand rubbed up and down my arm, setting a fire and putting out a different one, all in one gesture. "Now, do me favor. Let's put your engagement ring on . . . I never got to do it the other night. Then we need to get Weezie and smooth this over."

He shoved his hand in his pocket and brought out the ring he'd offered me the other night, like I was a done deal.

"I'm asking again, Shell, will you marry me?"

Waving a hand around aimlessly, I stammered, "I–I can't promise it'll be easy. What with my past, and clearly, my kid is a handful, and I don't know if this is over."

"I love you. I don't care. We're in this together," he said.

Slipping the ring on my finger, Cal kissed me and held me close to his side until there was a knock on the door.

Someone called out, "What's going on here today?"

"That's Jack," Cal said, squeezing my shoulder gently. "I needed him to drop something off for Weez. Can you get her?"

Typical Cal, calm and collected, had this whole scenario worked out in his head, and all was going to plan.

I side-eyed him, having a bad feeling about this delivery being more bribery. "She needs a stern talking-to, not packages."

"It was an emergency," Cal said, heading to the door.

I pushed to my feet and called out to my daughter from the bottom of the stairs. "Weez, can you come here?"

She came slowly down the stairs, then rushed to give me a hug. "I'm sorry, Mom, but I was scared."

"And you didn't call *Abuela*?"

"I didn't want to scare her. Cal's better." Without waiting for my response, she bounced on her way to the door. Apparently, my little one had more in common with Cal than Ricky.

When she wrapped her arms around the man of the hour, he said, "Hey, baby girl. Everything's all right. Say hi to Jack."

My daughter smiled at Jack, waving hello, and then of course, asked, "What's that?" eyeing the stack of boxes on my front porch.

"Jack brought these over for you, Weezie. They're from Ry, Adam, and me, welcoming you to the family."

"This man . . ." I growled for real this time.

Cal turned and shook his head at me, signaling for me to let it go.

"Can I open them?" Weezie asked him.

"Ask your mom," Cal had the sense to tell her.

She looked at me, and when I nodded, Jack and Cal carried the boxes inside.

"Hey, Shell," Jack said.

"Hey, Jack."

"Anything else?" he asked Cal, who told him to go enjoy the rest of his day.

Weezie was already ripping open boxes, making a royal mess, and shouting, "Look!"

In front of her was a huge American Girl doll haul. Clothes, a million toys to play with while using the doll, and a new baby with accessories were scattered all over my small living room.

"I have my own baby," she yelled, her braids whipping around. "A baby."

I started to say something, but Cal put his arm around me and kissed my temple.

"All's going to be good, darling," he whispered.

"Sometime in the last week, I went from *babe* to *darling*," I said, grinning at him.

"Making an honest woman out of you."

I punched Cal's arm, and he ignored me before going to help Weezie open boxes.

# EPILOGUE ONE

*Cal*

"Happy Thanksgiving," I said to Adam over FaceTime.

"Would be nice to be together, but glad we're not," he joked.

He and Rylan were celebrating Thanksgiving in Michigan with my mom. Their baby was due in a couple of weeks, and they'd decided their baby was going to be born in the States.

Shell and I planned on the opposite. I'd flown to the Caymans a week ago and would be here through all the holidays, including the New Year. Shell was a few days away from her due date, and I wasn't going to lie . . . panic had set in for me.

"Call us as soon as Shell goes into labor," Rylan hollered in the background. "Don't wait."

"Do what you want," Adam said, chuckling. "Have your baby and let us know when you want."

My brother knew I was turning into a bit of a basket case. It wasn't that I didn't want it all—Shell, Weezie, the new baby, marriage. It was my lack of self-confidence that I would be good at any of it.

"Let us know right away," my mom called out, chiming in.

"I'll let you all know when I can. Marva's going to come and stay with Weezie if Shell goes into labor in the middle of the night, but she made us promise to take them both to the waiting room if it happens during the day."

"That's my kind of girl. Knows what she wants," my mom said.

Mom was here last month after Shell and I told her we were engaged. Of course, my mom and Marva became fast friends, plotting a trip to New York after Shell and I moved there.

But Weezie was my mom's new BFF. Those two sat for hours playing dolls and games, talking and laughing. Weezie really brought out the best in her.

"Oh. Hi, Adam." Shell appeared next to me, speaking into the iPad. "I spoke with that manufacturer, and it seems like it's going to work out."

Adam had found Shell a facility in New Jersey to produce her syrups stateside, so she didn't have to deal with exporting them to the US from Grand Cayman.

"Good. Now, worry about having yourself a baby and then getting married."

"First, I need to make an American Thanksgiving," Shell joked.

"Cal isn't making you cook, is he? I know that . . ." Adam trailed off as Marva and Sam walked into the rental house, calling out, "Hello!"

"*Abuela*!" Weezie came running out in a swimsuit, her newest doll in tow. "Mom said I could swim when you got here."

"She did?"

"Cal's on the phone, and I'm too big to jump in after her," Shell said.

"Darling, I'll do it," I told Shell. I was getting better at swimming patrol.

"Sit," Marva said, and followed Weezie outside.

We'd moved into the rental house for the next few months, and put Shell's place up for sale. We agreed that whatever she received for it, we'd put into a college fund for Weezie.

As people strolled in and out of the house during the call, Adam took all the FaceTime interruptions in stride.

"We ordered dinner from the Grand," I told Adam, knowing everyone at his house were all listening. "They're coming soon to deliver and serve it."

Defending me, Rylan said, "Of course you did. Are they sending over the desserts to sample for the wedding reception too?" When Shell nodded into the camera, Rylan said, "I need you to tell me your thoughts."

Those two started talking pastries with my mom, and I told Adam, "Love ya, bro. I'm going outside."

"See you next year," he said.

Shell and I planned to get married in a very quick ceremony right after the baby was born, enabling her to move to the States with me. With Adam and Rylan's baby due so close after us, we decided to put off a bigger wedding until spring. This way, they could travel back to the Caymans with their baby and be here with all of us. Rylan was planning to have it at the Grand.

The only problem was my mom, who was going to miss the birth of our baby because of Adam's baby, but I reminded her as often as I could that he was her favorite. She shushed me and said she would be here in a few weeks before we moved back to the States.

It was all a complicated endeavor, but worth it. My assistant was enjoying my working virtually, probably sitting with his feet up on my desk.

"Cal, look!" Weezie jumped into the pool, and I looked up right away. I held up ten fingers when she surfaced, before sitting down next to Sam.

"All the paperwork is signed and filed," I told him.

Sam nodded. "I'm grateful."

"If he shows up, he'll not only be violating a restraining order, but also his lack of parental rights."

Another nod from Sam. "You did good. Now, make my daughter happy, every day."

Happy to agree, I grinned. "Every damn day."

# EPILOGUE TWO

• December, a year later •

*Shell*

"Mommy! Mommy, look!" Weezie said, bouncing on the bed and then shaking my shoulder.

"What time is it?" I choked out.

"Nine."

"Nine?" I bolted upright. "Where's Benjamin? Did you hear him cry? You have school." Sweat broke out on the nape of my neck as I swiped the hair out of my face.

"Mom, he's with Cal."

"Cal? It's Wednesday. He should be at work."

"Yeah, but we got snow. Look!" She jumped off the bed and went to open the blinds. "See?"

Pure white blanketed the sky and rooftops. Standing, I nodded in her direction and pulled a robe on, tying it around my waist. Snagging my phone off the nightstand, I confirmed the time and noted there were no messages from the coffee shop, which made me wonder if they'd opened on time.

"Beautiful," I whispered, standing behind my daughter at the window, taking in the scenery in front of us.

"That's what I think," I heard from directly behind me.

Cal's lips grazed my neck. Unfortunately, he didn't linger long because someone was pulling on my hair.

Turning around, I took in my husband in jeans and a navy sweater, our son in his arms, dressed in a snowsuit. "First off, why are you still home? Second, why is our son wearing a snowsuit . . . inside?"

"Cal made pancakes," my daughter said, and I noticed a smudge of syrup in the corner of her mouth.

"I even remembered the touch of coconut syrup," Cal said, winking.

"Is this a dream? You cooked? You're home and not at work?"

"I called the coffee shop. They're up and running. Pure genius hiring a manager who lived around the corner. Patrick said they're busy dealing with people who trekked out to see the snow. As for Amber, she'll come later after the roads are cleared and she can get the bus easily, so don't worry about the mess. She'll clean."

"Stop, I'm perfectly capable," I said, taking a grabby Benjamin. I shook my head, still not knowing what was going on. "Thanks for calling the shop. I don't want any bad reviews about us possibly opening late, but for the record, I can clean on my own," I told Cal, knowing he wouldn't agree. Adjusting to life with a full-time housekeeper was still a challenge a year later. "You know what? Let's start with the snowsuit."

Laying Benjamin down on the bed, I took off the suit, revealing a thermal onesie and flannel pants. Clucking my tongue, I said, "He's going to roast."

"I was worried he'd be cold. Remember when he was born, we had to keep that beanie on his head?"

Poor Cal, he tried, but he was a nervous Nellie when it came to parenting. I almost laughed out loud when I remembered how he'd jumped in the pool after Weezie that day at the Grand.

"He's fine, babe," I said to Cal. "He's one. He's going to walk soon, like a real person. But thank you for taking good care of him and Weez."

"He had oatmeal with mashed-up apples. Although most of it is on the wall."

I chuckled. Our boy was a messy eater.

"I let you sleep in," Cal said, stealing Benjamin off the bed and holding him tightly to his chest. "I'm working from home this morning, and I figured you needed the rest after last night." He sneaked in a wink at me.

"Can I watch TV?"

I started to say no to Weezie, but Cal beat me to it with a firm yes.

"It's a snow day, babe. That's what we do back east. Later, you can take her out to play in the snow."

The night before, Cal and I had shared a bottle of wine after both kids went to sleep. We exchanged Christmas gifts, even though it was only December twentieth.

This year, we planned to do Hanukkah and Christmas with Adam, Rylan, baby Becca, Ruth, and my parents at the Grand. We were leaving in a few days but wanted to share our own time together.

Cal got me earrings shaped like seashells, of course, but outlined in emeralds. I said they were too much, especially with my engagement ring and shell wedding band. I couldn't wear any of it to work, I told him. He argued and then shut his mouth when I kissed him.

Then I gave him his present . . . it was a picture of a Jeep. I'd bought Cal his very own Jeep to use when he wanted to get out of the city. After a lot of discussion, Cal and I decided I couldn't get to the Caymans as much as Rylan and Adam. New York was where Cal worked, and he needed to be here most of the time. Weezie was in a great school and making friends, and I couldn't pull her out as I wished. Plus, I loved my job, but mostly, I didn't like being away from Cal.

A few months ago, we put a bid on a place in the Hamptons. It wasn't the Caribbean, but it reminded me of home, with its salty air in the summer months and sand to run my toes through. I figured the Jeep would be more fun to take us there than a chauffeured car, and judging by Cal's response to my gift, he agreed.

His lips immediately locked with mine before his hands made quick work of my silk pajamas.

"Thank you, baby," he'd murmured before slinking down my body and showing his appreciation with his mouth.

Fast forward to this morning . . . and the chaos ensuing.

"Cal! The remote isn't working," Weezie called from the other room.

Sometimes she called him Daddy and others, Cal. We just rolled with it. She knew Ricky was out of her life for good and Cal was working toward legally adopting her. She owned Cal's heart and he ruled hers, but he wanted it to be official. Occasionally, she asked about Ricky and worried if he was okay. Mostly, though, Weezie said she was lucky to have found Cal for us when he jumped in the pool after her.

The timeline was a bit rough for her, and we didn't bother to straighten her out.

Cal and I ended up canceling the Caymans celebration (no offense to Rylan) and had a Sunday daytime wedding on the rooftop of a restaurant close to where we lived. Surrounded by our small family and a few friends, we said our vows, and then we all had brunch. It was the perfect way to have a wedding with one grade-schooler and two babies involved.

Weezie was a beautiful flower girl in both of our weddings, opting to stand next to Cal under the *chuppah*, and she even went up in a chair during the *hora* too at our party.

Of course, since we didn't get married until after Benjamin Lee arrived, he was a part of everything too. His middle name was meant to match Weezie's real name, Louise, at her request. Of course, she begged to carry him down the aisle at the second wedding, but we said no. He sat with Ruth, next to Rylan and Becca, drooling during the ceremony as both my parents walked me down the aisle.

Weezie loved Benjamin and asked every day if we could have more babies. She usually asked Cal because he never said no to her.

More babies were one of the reasons I paid my manager at Island Girl Outpost so well. After all, I'd be out on a maternity leave in about seven and a half months.

I was sure it would be hard staying away from my signature coffee shop in the West Village, but I knew Cal would insist I take a maternity leave. In only six months, we had a loyal following, mostly musicians from the neighboring universities, thanks to the open mic night and the weekly steel drum band.

The liquor license was what made us special. From four o'clock on, we offered boozy coffees with the syrups and had a small dessert menu featuring fried plantains, which brought in a lot of the arts crowd and professors.

"Coming," Cal said to Weezie and kissed my cheek.

I was left holding Benjamin, who was squirming to get down and move. When I set him on the floor, he half crawled, half walked to the window and pressed his sticky fingers on the glass so he could watch the snow.

"Ma," he called, and I went to him. Benjamin was a beautiful baby with a headful of curls and chubby cheeks, and dark brown eyes with a few of his daddy's golden flecks.

"It's snow, sweetie. We didn't have snow where I grew up," I told him, kneeling on the floor next to him.

"Ma," he said.

"Yep, little guy, I'm your Ma."

"She's all set." Cal came back in and knelt next to me, holding a mug of coffee. "For you."

"Half-caff?" I asked.

He nodded.

"Ugh, do you have to be so strict?"

He pulled me into his side and kissed my temple. "I certainly do."

"Da." Benjamin interrupted our moment, and I took a long sip of coffee.

"Hey, buddy. Should we take Mom to get some pancakes?"

"You should," I said, nodding enthusiastically.

"Come on."

We stood, Cal lifting Benjamin, and headed for the kitchen.

"You need to go to work," I told Cal.

"I will. Soon. I'm enjoying the moment."

Sitting down, I smirked, pushing my curly hair out of my eyes. "Look at that, the party boy has settled down into domestic bliss."

Cal winked and got in the last word. "I can still party with the best of them. Before nine o'clock."

# ACKNOWLEDGMENTS

In an effort to keep these brief and not leave anyone out, much thanks to Pam, Virginia, Sarah, the Tippetts gang, Valentine PR/Grey's Promo, Nic, Christy, Fab, beta readers extraordinaire, all my friends, family, and my dogs for putting up with me during this process.

# ABOUT THE AUTHOR

Rachel Blaufeld is a bestselling author of Romantic Suspense, New Adult, Coming-of-Age Romance, and Sports Romance. A recent poll of her readers described her as *insightful*, *generous*, *articulate*, and *spunky*. Originally a social worker, Rachel creates broken yet redeeming characters. She's been known to turn up the angst like cranking up the heat in the dead of winter.

A devout coffee drinker and doughnut eater, Rachel spends way too many hours in local coffee shops, downing the aforementioned goodies while she plots her ideas. Her tales may all come with a side of angst and naughtiness, but end as lusciously as her treats.

As a side note, Blaufeld, also a long-time blogger and an advocate of woman-run anything, is fearless about sharing her opinion. To her, work/life/family balance is an urban legend, but she does her best.

Rachel has also blogged for *The Huffington Post*, *Modern Mom*, and *USA TODAY*, where she shared conversations at "In Bed with a Romance Author" and reading recommendations at "Happy Ever After."

Rachel lives around the corner from her childhood home in Pennsylvania with her family and two beagles. Her obsessions include running, coffee, basketball, icing-filled doughnuts, antiheroes, and mighty fine epilogues.

To connect with Rachel, she's most active in her private reading group, *The Electric Readers*, where she shares insider information and intimate conversation with her readers:

Tunnel VIPs

As well as:
www.rachelblaufeld.com
Twitter
Facebook
Newsletter

If you liked this book, feel free to leave a review where you bought it or on Goodreads. Send me an e-mail when you do, and I will thank you personally!

www.ingramcontent.com/pod-product-compliance
Lightning Source LLC
Chambersburg PA
CBHW070507260626
47161CB00004B/1486